Thank you
for Everything!

An Enchanted Life

You're the best neighbour ever!!

An Adept's Guide to Masterful Magick

Con mucho cariño

Luis y Serafin

By
Patricia Telesco

NEW PAGE BOOKS
A division of The Career Press, Inc.
Franklin Lakes, NJ

AN ENCHANTED LIFE

Edited by Dianna Walsh
Typeset by Kristen Mohn
Cover design by Cheryl Cohan Finbow
Illustrations by Colleen Koziara
Printed in the U.S.A. by Book-mart Press

To order this title, please call toll-free 1-800-CAREER-1 (NJ and Canada: 201-848-0310) to order using VISA or Master Card, or for further information on books from Career Press.

The Career Press, Inc., 3 Tice Road, PO Box 687,
Franklin Lakes, NJ 07417
www.careerpress.com
www.newpagebooks.com

Library of Congress Cataloging-in-Publication Data

Telesco, Patricia, 1960-
  An enchanted life : an adept's guide to masterful magick / by Patricia Telesco.
    p. cm.
  Includes bibliographical references and index.
  ISBN 1-56414-566-2
    1. Magic. 2. Spiritual life. I Title

BF1621 .T42 2001
133.4'3--dc21

2001044366

This book is lovingly dedicated to the "crazy, water-witching indian," his lovely wife Deena, "she who giggles," and their merry band of family and friends. Thank you for welcoming me to your sacred fire with such warmth and hospitality. May the love you radiate reach out and bless All our Relations.
Aho!

Contents

Preface

*"My mother says I must not pass too near that glass;
she is afraid that I will see a little witch that looks
like me."*

—Sarah Morgan Bryant Piatt

Some 15 years ago as of this writing, I discovered that down deep in my spirit, beneath layers of societal, familial, and cultural teachings, there lived a witch! This came as a total and complete surprise to me. After all, I grew up in the Lutheran faith, spent five years as a Pentecostal missionary, spent a few more years in an agnostic haze, and then stumbled on New Age thinking quite innocently.

What came as an even greater surprise was the realization that my journey wasn't that unique or odd. In fact, there were thousands of people just like me who discovered alternative spirituality in much the same way, with equal surprise and delight. For all of us, it was like coming home to something you'd believed all along, but for which you had no name.

The wonder and blessing of that discovery still lingers in my heart and mind. Nonetheless, the witch within me isn't quite the same as she was in the beginning. I'm not so prone to taking the easy road, not so anxious to use formulaic spells, not so hesitant about creating my own traditions; I am much more interested in how our diversity makes us strong and hopefully much wiser overall. So, where does all this leave me and the others who have walked the magickal road for many a year?

The answer to that question isn't an easy one. Since the 1970s, Wicca and neo-paganism have been taking baby steps forward into becoming "adult" religions. In the process, there have been many magickal practitioners who have left their figurative spiritual diapers in the compost heap. Consequently, we are weary of basic "101," milk-toast, fluffy-bunny writings. We yearn for something deeper, something that will help us continue our path toward metaphysical maturity.

The time for such things to come to pass is overdue. It is my sincere prayer that this book represents one such effort. In reading that last statement, however, please know that I do not consider myself an "adept." To me, adepthood isn't necessarily a proverbial brass ring that you just reach one day, and then that's the end of it. Instead, it's an ongoing series of goals, internalized wisdoms, accepted responsibilities, failures, reevaluations, and accomplishments that do not end until the end of life itself (and even beyond). So if you're looking for a book that will make you an all-commanding, all-knowing, all-powerful Wiccan or neo-pagan who puts Samantha Stevens (of the 1960s' *Bewitched* television program) to shame, look elsewhere.

If, however, you want a helpmate in your quest to become a more proficient, accountable, trustworthy, and respectable member of the magickal community, then I believe you're in the right place. Why? Because I have the same goal as you do, and I would like to use these pages as a way to begin walking toward that goal together. At least one of the lessons of adepthood boils down to the simple words: We need each other.

Let's move forward along our Path with confidence so that a variety of positive spiritual traditions can continue to have a viable public face and the freedom to worship. What we plant today will root and grow, not just in our spirits but in the world.

Introduction

*"It is not only by the questions we have answered
that progress may be measured but also by those
we are still asking."*

—Freda Adler

Gather 'round the sacred fire and be welcome. Bring with you all your life's lessons, stories, and songs, and celebrate them. Sit with others of a like mind, Spirit, and this book, all of which indicate your desire to do more than simply file away the magickal moments of your life into some dusty cabinet. You want to apply them, internalize them, and keep moving forward. That is as it should be, because living an enchanted life is all about challenging ourselves, learning, achieving, honoring, and then starting again at a new challenge. The cycle does not end.

Nonetheless, because metaphysical traditions are relatively young in terms of having a coherent, public image, there isn't a lot of helpful material available to further our spiritual growth. Additionally, I often fear that many of us spend too much time focusing and worrying about the path we've taken to enlightenment. If we are always thinking about *how* we practice, instead of remembering *why* we do so, we will never achieve enchanted living. The "how" is superficial; the "why" is transformational.

With this in mind, *An Enchanted Life* was written to help you progress spiritually without becoming stagnant, falling into common traps, getting overly discouraged, or giving in to boxy thinking. Spirit cannot be confined to a neat container; in other words, we cannot remake God/dess in our image, even though that is the way of humankind. Similarly, your spiritual development is something very personal, and it can't be confined or quantified in any box or book!

So, for a little while I would ask you to try and set aside preconceived notions of what qualifies as being spiritually adept, and just be. Go through this book with an open mind and soul, letting the personally meaningful philosophies and activities work through you and into you. And at the end, begin again!

Enchanted living is not about reaching any one pinnacle. It's not about being more powerful. If anything, it's about responsibility. Culpability requires that we not simply "talk the good talk" but really walk the walk, every moment of every day, transforming even the most mundane of chores into magickal moments and memories. It is with that awareness that *An Enchanted Life* begins by stopping to honor the Path that brought you to this critical crossroad in your journey. We cannot know where we are going without first understanding where we have been and why.

Next, *An Enchanted Life* takes you on an adventure through the senses, each of which you can hone and heighten to serve your spirit and magick more effectively. Our senses are not simply a medium for understanding the temporal world. They can open whole new avenues for understanding and interpreting the spirit realms too!

Finally, we come to the lion's share of the book: The Way, the Path: The Ends and Means. Here, I present four potential avenues for personal growth, which together can also become a powerful whole. These are the Paths of Healer, Teacher, Warrior, and Visionary, titles that almost anyone who seriously practices a metaphysical art will (at some point or another) have to embrace temporarily or forever.

As you read these chapters, you'll notice I've provided 50 practices for enchanted living, which are listed in their entirety on pages 16 to 19 at the end of this introduction. These are meant to be like the black-and-white outlines in a spiritual coloring book to which you bring the crayons of your imagination and vision. While not hard and fast rules, these concepts provide a sound foundation on which to build any spiritual practice.

Of course, I'm not declaring these practices or this specific process to be the only effective approaches for those wishing to take the next steps in their spiritual sojourn. Instead, I'm sharing various global insights into methods that have proven effective for me (the "fly-by-the-seat-of-her-broomstick" witch), and individuals in many other traditions. To this foundation you can, and should, bring your own voice, beliefs, and ethics. This will give you a meaningful system for transformation in which you have always remained as the proverbial co-pilot.

We are the masters of our destiny. We have all the tools within us to reach our spiritual goals successfully. All that's missing is the key to unlocking those tools. My sincere wish is that this book becomes a key for you, one that opens the doors of potential and possibility in whole new ways. Before you begin, I would like to leave you with these words adapted from a beautiful Gaelic prayer:

God/dess guide you, and sustain you.
God/dess stand before you as an example and
behind you to protect.
God/dess live with you, inspire you, and direct your
journey as you walk on the Path, and Spirit abides
in your steps.

Fair Winds and Sweet Water in your travels.

50 Practices for Enchanted Living

1. Live in the moment and fully appreciate its worth.
2. Balance and support all aspects of self and one's environment into a harmonious whole.
3. Acknowledge the results of your efforts in a special way that encourages integration.
4. Honor yourself and remember to be your own best friend.
5. Believe in your importance in both the mundane and magickal realms.
6. Know thyself in truthfulness.
7. Work for the good of all; do the best, right thing.
8. Recognize when you have a need and find a way to fulfill it.
9. Appraise your paths and beliefs regularly to make sure they still fit the transformations in and around you.
10. Practice what you preach.
11. Keep modesty as a companion and guide.

12. Give something back.
13. Know that in magick, a symbol is every bit as powerful as what it represents.
14. Remember that things don't have to be complicated to work.
15. Know that meaning is everything.
16. Always make room for spirit and soul-fullness in your life.
17. See that life is an act of worship; you are the magick.
18. Understand that without mental focus and fortitude in the tangible present, very little will happen metaphysically in the future.
19. Recognize that you are your own best guru and guide.
20. Improvise and practice, practice, practice.
21. Always work with intention.
22. Remember that patterns equal power, realization, and manifestation when treated respectfully and applied sensitively.
23. Know that spirituality is not about keeping up with anyone else. The only real gauge for growth lies in the altar of your heart.
24. Don't expect anyone else to do something that you, yourself, are not willing to accept or do.
25. You have to know where you've been to glean a vision for where you're going.
26. Remember and honor wholeness, which helps you begin to make your way back to wholeness.
27. Know that everything in magick begins in thought and fullness.

28. Understand that each of us participates in our destiny, but only you can determine how much you create and how much you allow.

29. Dare to dream, then make your dreams come true.

30. Accept your weaknesses gracefully and honor your talents with equal poise; then work on both!

31. Take your senses and your spirituality out of the box.

32. Don't work magick if you don't want responsibility.

33. Don't put on airs. Dare to let down the walls to laugh, to cry, to *be* human.

34. Always clean up your messes.

35. Never underestimate the power of a life lived differently.

36. Be willing to learn and be open to new experiences.

37. Do not try to be anyone else's guru.

38. Remember that unapplied knowledge is wasteful (if not tragic).

39. Use it, appreciate it, or lose it!

40. Cultivate the mind of perfect love.

41. Understand that humor is good soul food.

42. Recognize that the universe always uses the best skill sets we have for the task at hand to effect change.

43. Remember that proactive, positive thoughts and words lead to proactive, positive magick!

44. Maintain a poised, positive bearing; it goes a long way toward making your case for you.

45. Respect the temple of self; treat your body, mind, and spirit as a sacred thing.

46. Believe that we are children of the universe and people of power.

47. Understand that there are no limits to magick and our spirits other than those we create.

48. Have fun with your Magick. Tinker, tweak, then try!

49. Know that hard work is good magick.

50. Live the other 49 practices, and be yourself!

Part I:

Honoring the Journey

"On life's journey, faith is nourishment, virtuous deeds are a shelter, wisdom is the light by day, and right mindfulness is the protection by night."

—Buddha

"In the arena of human life the honors and rewards fall to those who show their good qualities in action."

—Aristotle

Chapter 1

The Book of You

"Every action of our lives touches on some chord that will vibrate in eternity."
—Edwin Hubbel Chapin

The Path to enchanted living and adepthood is forever transforming beneath our feet. It grows and changes with us, with the earth, and with the universe. That means staying on our toes, being honest in our motivations, being aware, remaining steadfast, and living in a way that honors each part of the journey to our awakening. In particular, as we achieve specific goals or reach critical junctures in our learning/training, we need to stop long enough to celebrate and integrate what has occurred; otherwise, an important foundational step is overlooked. With this in mind, think of this chapter as a pausing point in your spiritual sojourn. This acts as an opportunity to celebrate the "book of you" as it's been written to this point, reinforce the solid spiritual foundations that have been constructed thus far, and then continue building on that joy and certainty throughout the years ahead.

TRANSFORMATIVE MOMENTS

*"Only one thing has to change for us to know
happiness in our lives: where we focus our attention."*
—Greg Anderson

Every life is composed of moments joined together. With the hectic pace of most people's lives, many important moments in this composition, especially the ones that make us who and what we are, get overlooked. This needs to change. Why? Because the proverbial Golden Rule for enchanted living (Practice 1, page 16) is not only living in the moment, but fully appreciating its worth.

To give a personal example, I recently had the chance to visit some friends. The weather was beautiful and the company warm and welcoming. Nonetheless, a little gray cloud hovered over me due to some problems back home. Rather than reveling in the pleasure of good companions, I allowed the problems to become my focus. By so doing, I missed a lot of the good, refreshing moments that visit could have held for me.

Now, I'm not beating myself up about this. What I did was normal, but it wasn't wise. Rather than clinging to frustration, I should have shared it, then moved on, releasing myself to that moment and its power. Then I would have come home renewed and ready to tackle things instead of feeling tired before I began! I'm sure I'm not the only person to have experienced situations like this, and it is but one good illustration of why enchanted living is moment-to-moment living.

Activity 1.1: Improving Awareness of the Moment
For this activity, I want you to get a timer and set it for one hour. Do this when you can wholly

devote yourself to that hour with few interruptions. Once the timer is set, go about doing whatever you need to do, but instead of just going through the motions, pay attention. Ask yourself some questions:

* In what direction are you moving?
* What is your personal ritual for this part of the day?
* What, of that ritual, empowers you or improves your outlook?
* Are you doing anything destructive or unproductive that could be changed?
* How do you feel in your skin: comfortable, ill-at-ease?
* How is your breathing? Is it deep and connected or hurried?
* What items in your environment catch your eye regularly? Are they things that uplift you and celebrate your Path?

Basically, I'm asking you to pay attention to everything. The way you sit and stand, the way you interact with your environment, and the way all these things affect you. If you repeat this activity in various locations once a day for a week or once a week for a couple of months, I can guarantee your awareness of the moment will improve. As it does, you will be able to make better use of any transitional moments by adding magickal and spiritual techniques into the equation.

Each Moment Matters

Now, I should note at this juncture that living presently and attentively doesn't throw out forethought as unimportant or unnecessary. It simply says that while our tomorrows will come (and we should be prepared for them), we are *here, now!* Once this moment passes, you can't get it back! And because the future is built on the past, each moment matters, mundanely and spiritually. This brings me to Practice 2 (page 16) of enchanted living, which works cooperatively with living in the now; that is, maintaining balance and symmetry.

Just as we cannot hang onto the past forever, or look so much to the future than we never accomplish anything today, we also cannot forget that adept living acknowledges the whole person. You are not simply spirit. You have body and mind, and you live in a very real world. All of these facets of self and the environment have to be acknowledged and supported for someone to truly claim enchanted living 24 hours a day, seven days a week.

Activity 1.2: Bringing Magick to Mundania, and Vice Versa

When we look at our day-to-day lives, it's often hard to see the magick there, or to find ways to bring magick into each moment. I don't know about anyone else, but I hardly feel spiritual before my first cup of coffee, let alone after a night with a sick child, a day of office politics, or hours in a traffic jam. Nonetheless, each of these situations, each of these moments is part of a greater whole, a whole to which we're trying to bring positive energy for enchanted living!

For this activity, I'd like you to make a list of 10 very mundane things you have to do daily or weekly: in other words, things that you don't think of as remotely spiritual. Leave yourself a lot of free space in between each item where you can do free-flow writing. If need be, put each of the 10 on a separate piece of paper.

Once a day during the next 10 days, take one of those items at random when you have 30 to 45 minutes to ponder it. Think about what it may symbolize on a metaphysical level. For example, brushing my teeth (to me) equates to "clean" communications—the purity and power of words. Then consider how you might apply that symbolism to empower the moment. In this example, I might choose mint toothpaste on a day when I have to communicate about financial matters effectively because one of the metaphysical correspondences for mint is money!

Do you see how this example takes an everyday action and turns it into productive spiritual time? If you follow through with all 10 of the items on your list, and try the applications, I can promise your life will transform in very real and exciting ways. You will find yourself approaching old and new tasks alike with a creative, spiritual eye, an eye that appreciates the potential in that moment (Practice 1, page 16).

Recognize the Results

In appreciating moments and keeping our lives in balance, another key guideline comes to bear: acknowledgment.

While we might see the potential in the moment, and even keep things on an even keel, if we never stop to acknowledge the results of those two things working in tandem, we've missed a vital opportunity. So, the Practice 3 (page 16) of enchanted living is to stop, look, recognize, and integrate the results of our efforts.

When we stop moving, we also give Spirit a chance to get our attention. When we look and truly *see*, the soul grasps a new vision, one of wholeness. When we recognize and integrate the importance of our vision, it transforms our lives from the inside out.

Activity 1.3: Marking Magickal Moments

This activity is an ongoing one that you should set your mind to for at least six months. During that time, carry a small notebook with you everywhere. When a special moment happens, and you sense the Universe giving you a gift or a lesson, write it down. Put as much detail into your writing as time and circumstances allow.

Once a month, read these entries in a quiet place where you won't be interrupted (turn off the phone; honest, they'll call back!). Ponder what that moment meant to you, how it shifted your thinking or being in some way. If you had to narrow that whole experience down to a few key words, what would they be? For example, in the previous example of visiting friends the key words might have been:

Release

Be Joyful Now

Really, that was the entire lesson in a nutshell, but what a lesson! It may be some time before I can live that lesson, but it is now part of me, and I have acknowledged it. The moment of acknowledgment is where internalization begins.

By the way, keep this little diary going if you can. You will find it becomes a great companion with whom you can share your intimate thoughts freely, and who will share them back to you whenever you have need. Read it on your birthday, a magickal anniversary, or any time you just want to watch your own progress.

Honor Yourself

Speaking of birthdays, anniversaries, and other similar occasions, remember that these are part of acknowledgment too. Our life is a sacred wheel. Moments like the date of our birth, and that of our initiation, are spokes that drive the wheel forward. They are the lines of force in who we are. When you honor that line and celebrate these things, you give each spoke greater strength and weight, making you a similarly stronger, more assured individual. Practice 4 (page 16) is a very good rule for enchanted living: Honor yourself and remember to be your own best friend.

To illustrate this point, I will tell you that I tend to brush off my birthday a lot. I used every excuse in the book: I'm busy, I'm tired, it's not important, and so on. But the reality was that deep down I didn't think I'd earned a celebration, that somehow I wasn't worthy of that time and jubilation. Effectively, I broke that spoke in self's sacred wheel and had to rebuild it.

How did I begin fixing that spoke? I reached out to some friends and asked them to help me create an all-out gala, which jokingly became known as the Trish-a-nallia (because the date falls near a Bacchus festival). I cannot remember a time in my life when I felt so vital and happy. For that moment, I was the center of my entire life's wheel and everyone there revolved around that point, not because they had to, but because they wanted to.

Now that might sound egotistical, but we need our egos. They help us in many aspects of life, and too many spiritual beings give in to the "I'm not important" mind-set. This robs them of their power, of the self-awareness that Practice 3 (page 16) tries to create. So, Practice 5 is: To live an empowered spiritual life you must truly believe that you are important, your vision is important, and your unique way of reflecting spirit is important. However you decide to maintain that self-assurance in your life is really up to you, but stopping long enough for acknowledgment certainly helps.

PROFICIENCY AND POWER

> *"The point of power is always in the present."*
> —Louise L. Hay

As an adept lives in the moment, he or she must also be a master over self, and then over her craft. This means having hands-on experience with all of the traditional tools and methods of magick, and then choosing from among those the ones in which you wish to excel. Each person has a gift that the universe wants to use. The adept's task is discovering that gift and then honing it until it glows!

This section will help you begin finding the area in which you should concentrate, not just in magick but in life (see also

Practice 2)! The first step in that process is focusing on Practice 6 (page 16): Know thyself in truthfulness. If you don't know who you are, from where you've come, or where you hope to go, you can never live a truly enchanted existence. Magick is knowledge, knowledge is power, and power is responsibility. Without knowledge of self, magick often dies (or minimally falters like a fish out of water).

Over the years, and especially when we're under long-term stress, the sense of identity can be lost. Somewhere within you know and honor your talents, instincts, and strengths. You also recognize areas that need improvement. Both of these parts of self have to be examined honestly if you want to work magick responsibly.

For example, perhaps you identify great compassion as one of your strengths and clinginess as one of your weaknesses. Someone with this profile probably isn't the best candidate to work love magick for another. The result might be an overly giving love (e.g. compassion to a fault) or an overly possessive love (e.g. clingy). Because you are the enabler in magick, and the resulting energy flows through you, unless those aspects of self can be set aside or balanced out, they will naturally affect the energy you direct.

Activity 1.4 – Self-Awareness Check

How well do you know the sacred self? Who are you mundanely, physically, mentally, and spiritually? Who are some of the people you admire, and which of their characteristics would you like to see developed or augmented within? What aspects of yourself are you actively working to change (but still haven't mastered)? Make a list on a sheet of paper of both your positive and negative characteristics.

Next, consider how those negatives might affect your spiritual pursuits. Is there any type of process right now that you shouldn't undertake? For example, someone who feels insight is presently lacking probably won't want to offer to do divinatory readings for others until that problem is resolved. Next to each negative you've listed, write a word or phrase that indicates its potential impact.

Don't stop there and get discouraged. If you identify problems, you can also fix them! Now move to the positive list. Consider how all those characteristics blend together within you. What kind of proverbial cake do they make? Are you suited to serve, to teach, to organize, to motivate, to nurture? You should be able to distinguish some kind of theme from what you've listed. For example, someone who feels their positive characteristics include a motherly spirit, good communication skills, and natural healing aptitude is going to make an excellent nurturer or motivator, and possibly a facilitator! Where do you fit in? Find your place and celebrate!

Know Your Strengths and Needs

Honestly recognizing our strengths and limitations helps us work for the good of all, which is also a very good practice for enchanted living (Practice 7, page 16). I should note, however, that working for the good of all can (and often does) mean working for *you*. Even the wisest sage, the most adept guru, and the most insightful teacher cannot give their best to others if the inner well remains unattended. Slowly but surely, that well will go dry, and an important member of the community burns out. Don't let that happen.

Practice 8 (page 16) for enchanted living is to recognize when you have a need and then find a way to fulfill it, even if that just means saying no once in a while. Many individuals in our community are great givers, but they find it hard to receive because it seems selfish. It's not. If you cannot open yourself to receive, you will never truly know the wonder of giving. It is a marvelously balanced process that the universe flows through to hold, heal, and refresh us when we let it.

More amazing still is how many people are just waiting for you to ask for help! They've stood by silently, biting their tongues, and waiting to give something back. When you open that door you bless them as much as yourself. Start today!

Activity 1.5 - Giving to Yourself

Perpetual volunteers and workaholics will hate this activity! Stop for a moment, right there. Yes, in the middle of this book, just stop. Ask yourself: When was the last time you did something nice for you? When was the last time you reached out to a friend or loved one for support with a problem? Ah, no fibbing (Practice 6)! If it's been more than a few weeks, you're long overdue, so fix it.

Get up and go get yourself a treat, then call or visit someone you trust and respect and express at least one honest need. Let that person minister to you, even as you would give wholly to them. Begin refilling that inner well so that you work from a full glass instead of one that's empty and wanting. Don't feel selfish, don't apologize for being human; simply relax and allow. With time and a little practice, you'll find you can do this without inner struggle, and in turn be more refreshed for ministry and magick 24-7.

Evaluate Your Beliefs

So you're now feeling a little better about yourself in the whole scheme of things, especially spiritually. Now what? The next step is a fair appraisal of your belief system. Specifically, ask yourself:

* Which ethical guidelines does your faith or personal vows require of you?

* Which emotional, physical, and mental guidelines or challenges does your faith offer? In answering this, remember you are body, mind, and spirit; all three must be served to truly become adept at anything.

* What are the basic strictures of your beliefs and how flexible are they to meet the moment and a changing world?

* How do you see god (active, inactive, as one face, as many)?

* What is your view on other spiritual paths, even those with which you might not always agree? (While this question might make you uncomfortable, no fabrications or rose-colored glasses per Practice 6, page 16, are allowed.)

* How do you see your beliefs changing as time goes on, and will that affect by what "name" you call yourself (e.g. Wiccan, Buddhist, Pagan, Shaman...)?

* How do you see others in your faith changing as time goes on, and how will this affect the stability of the whole?

* Which role(s) do you see yourself accepting in your faith and why?

* What attracted you to your current belief system and does that factor still hold appeal?
* Has your faith grown and changed with you, or is it stagnating and potentially holding you back?
* Are you as happy now with your choice of Path as you were in the beginning? Why or why not?
* What will continue to make you happy or improve things?
* Does your belief system uplift and motivate the individual's potential or undermine it? How?
* Does your belief system uplift and motivate group potential or undermine it, and by extension humankind's potential?
* Does your belief system honor the Earth (versus viewing it as something over which to have dominion)?

Question Your Path

These questions are not easy to answer and will likely take some soul searching, perhaps even more so for those of us who have walked this road for a very long time. It's easy to get comfortable and complacent, to overlook that sense of wonderment we had when we first found our way, and to become indifferent to our blessings. With this in mind, Practice 9 (page 16) for enchanted living is to regularly ask yourself these questions. Appraise your Path as it was and is, and as it may be in the future. Make sure it is still right for you.

How will you know? There are several good indicators. If you haven't grown, changed, and been challenged in the last year, I'd say you're either on the wrong Path or sitting on your butt in the road; only you can honestly discern which. If the living of your life isn't speaking to people around you in some way, that's another good pointer. Being adept is about BE-ing the magick, and that's something people notice.

A third indicator that builds on the last is practicing what you preach (Practice 10, page 16). One cannot practice the rules of balance, acknowledgment, honor, recognition, belief, and truth and not follow this guideline. If you're not walking the walk, perhaps you're not walking the right Path. If you are, you are not walking the right way and need to make some serious changes before proceeding further in this book.

Activity 1.6 - What Do You Believe? What Do You Live?

Return to the previous question about the ethical, emotional, mental, and physical guidelines or challenges your faith presents. Make a list of them on a sheet of paper. Now, return to the process of the Self-Awareness Check (Activity 1.4, page 31), only use it this time to measure each guideline against your heart. Think of Maat, the Egyptian goddess of truth, and how she would use an ostrich feather to weigh a soul's heart on magickal scales. If the scales balanced, the soul would be filled with light and justice, and thus allowed to roam freely with gods and spirits alike. How does that guideline weigh against your actions?

If you come up with a negative response to any of those guidelines, the next question is, "Why?" Is it because in your heart and soul this is something with which you don't agree? If so, how important is that guideline to the Path: Is it a dividing boundary or a gray shading? If it is a boundary, you may have to rethink your foundations.

While we choose a Path, our feet mold the soil beneath us. As you walk, that Path shifts a bit with your movement in each step you take. As much as it changes you, you change it! And there may come a day when you outgrow that road and have to find one that goes to a slightly different place in spirit and life to become fulfilled and whole.

If you do agree with the guideline and still answer that you're not following it, then the question becomes: What in yourself resists this? Is it due to apathy, fear, insecurity, laziness, or an unwillingness to truly walk the walk, that is, wanting all the good stuff and none of the responsibility? Again, only you can answer this question, but realize that you also have the power to change the answer here if you so choose!

If you can think it, and trust in it, and act on it, you can be it, which in turn means your life will mirror your beliefs. Rather than bemoaning your fate, or wishing, just do: Fix it and turn that corner!

Appreciate the Universe's Gifts

Now, none of us are perfect (would that we were). We are going to mess up and even sometimes stray off our mark altogether. The important thing is knowing when we're straying so we can find our way back home again. It's also perfectly okay to admit when we're wrong or when we're unsure! That too is part of becoming an adept, and better still, it keeps us humble.

With an honest appraisal of self and your Path in hand, you can then start looking at what gifts the universe has given you, or those you might have the ability of acquiring in service of the All. Enchanted living recognizes that we need each other. That knowledge doesn't do much good, however, if each of us isn't aware of our spiritual potential. Even more so, we need to be working toward actualizing that potential in concrete ways or we can't truly help one another. Because Practice 12 (page 17) is, "Give something back"—to a person, to your craft, or to the world—it's easy to see why identifying and properly using gifts is important.

Generally speaking, I separate gifts into four categories, each of which seems to have a strong relationship with an Element. (Note: This association is purely personal observation on my part.) If you are aware of your personal power Element, you may find some correlation with the associated gifts, but not always! Because each of us blends the Elements in magick and in life, each of them can find some form of expression in the way the universe flows through us.

Also, bear in mind that the universe uses mundane talents as much as spiritual aptitude. I remember when I first meditated about writing and asked the simple question: Why me? At that time in my life I had no formal training in magick and not a whole lot of research material with which to work. The simple, and rather humbling, reply I got from the universe was "because you said yes, and you had the skills needed." So, basically I was in the right place, with the right mundane aptitude, at the right time, and gave the right answer! This kind of thing can happen to anyone who is open and willing.

Now that doesn't lessen your uniqueness or specialness (not everyone answers a call to their heart!). It just keeps things in perspective, which supports Practice 11 (page 16).

Keep modesty as a good companion and guide in your efforts to advance in your spiritual path. There will always be people ahead of you, behind you, and beside you. Those beside you become comrades, those behind you can be motivated by your success, and those ahead of you can inspire! Life is an ongoing learning process that does not end until you do, and because our spirit is eternal, the exact date on that is open for interpretation.

Emotional Gifts / Water (The Ebb and Flow of Feeling)

Emotional gifts include empathy, understanding, compassion, sensitivity, motivation, inspiration, and comfort. Many of people with emotional gifts struggle in their late teens and early 20s to control the feelings within, many of which don't even originate with self. As they get older, these people can become terminal volunteers, are easily drawn into other people's troubles, and often end up in careers with caregiving overtones.

Spiritually speaking, people with (or who wish to develop) emotional gifts make excellent:

* Diviners: They can deliver a message that's constructive (e.g. reveal even bad news in good ways), while also seeing past surface realities.
* Facilitators: Others are naturally inspired by their knack for getting inside people's heads and hearts.
* Counselors: They must, however, detach and cleanse afterward.
* Ministers: They serve heart, mind, and spirit; emoters have a natural understanding of holistics.
* Motivational speakers: They know all the right words for nearly any group, situation, or individual.

* Medics: They often intuitively see when something is wrong before it even happens.
* Trailblazers: Just as water adapts to fit any shape, these people know how to take things into the future with flexibility and innovation as a guide.

The main drawback in this profile is that emotional gifts can also sometimes enable others in negative behaviors. You will need to take care to do a self-check and really listen to your inner voice to know when to "jump in" and when to remain outside the situation.

Mental Gifts / Fire (The Light of the Mind)

Mental gifts include reasoning skills, comprehension, fast learning, scholarship, discernment (especially of cause-effect relationships), planning, and keen artistic or cultural perception (particularly of value). Many people with mental gifts struggle in their youth to fit in, always feeling older or smarter than those around them. As they get older, these individuals can become terminal students, are easily drawn into a life with books, and often end up in careers that have scholarly overtones.

Spiritually speaking, people with (or who wish to develop) mental gifts make excellent:

* Researchers: They can put the foundations under faith.
* Writers: They may need someone to edit their lofty notions, but there's a lot of knowledge here that can be shared.
* Talent Scouts: When an event organizer is looking for good merchants and artists, send these individuals out hunting. They will find the diamonds among the coal.

40

* Organizers: These people could reorder the government if given half the chance. Let them set up structure and things will go smoothly.
* Peacekeepers: The rational, balanced nature of these individuals allows them to see both sides of the equation, and often an equitable solution.
* Leaders (background): These people's natural ability to learn and pick out other talented people may thrust them into positions of leadership, but not always comfortably. If possible, they should stick to second-in-command roles and let someone else do the talking.
* Child-Care Coordinators: The lighthearted joy of our community's children is good soul food for the sometimes overly heady thinker. They will also immediately see a child's natural abilities and foster them.

The main drawback in this profile is that mentally gifted people can become trapped in thought and calculations rather than living in the moment. Also, their intelligence may impede effective communication to common people.

Spiritual Gifts / Air (The Whispering Wind)

Spiritual gifts include faith, psychism, conviction, an astral/mystical perception, arcane knowledge or talents, channeling, healing, and visions. Many people with spiritual gifts struggle in their youth because they feel outside of time and space somehow. As they get older, they may turn to a specific religious calling, study theology, or turn to a life of quiet introspection. Alternatively, they may try to turn off this connection altogether because of the intensity of awareness.

Spiritually speaking, people with (or who wish to develop) mental gifts make excellent:

* Ministers (of any belief): Ministers are called, not necessarily made, and this person has a definite mark on his or her spirit direct from the Divine for service.
* Holisticians use sensitivity to guide their patient toward body-mind-spirit balance.
* Counselors who listen with inner ears for signals and signs of trouble that a person may not otherwise reveal.
* Psychics who attune themselves to the world's (and not-world's) pulse for insights.
* Modern minded Mages/Alchemists.
* Facilitators who can guide events and the attendants into a communal experience for the good of all.

The main drawback with the spiritually gifted person is the temptation to retreat from the here and now, this world of concrete that they don't wholly understand. But in order to bring Spirit in the world, one cannot run away from it. The biblical saying, "Live in the world, but be not *of* it," comes to bear here.

Physical Gifts / Earth (The Soil of Growth)

Physical gifts include strength, durability, vitality, heartiness, and quick rejuvenation. As a young person, the physically gifted often become athletes, but also may push their bodies to harm. Additionally, because of the overall physical prowess, some may give into bullying as a way of impressing the will.

Spiritually speaking, people with (or who wish to develop) physical gifts make excellent helpmates. They can help those who are incapable perform chores, or give physical assistance to young and old alike. Specifically, in the setting of a festival or other spiritual event, these people are great "tote and bail" people whose assistance in setup, maintenance, and breakdown is invaluable.

PATTERNS OF POWER

> *"Continuing to cling to the patterns you know*
> *inhibits your ability to discover what you don't know."*
> — Eric Allenbaugh

Stop for a moment to look at the world's labyrinths, mandalas, mazes, glyphs, and sigils. Here we see that spiritual people throughout history, and in a variety of cultural settings, were trying to physically portray something significant to the universe and our very soul: the patterns of power. I truly believe an in-depth study of these, and learning to apply them effectively, will lead to improved results in our daily life and our magick.

All life, all energy consists of a specific pattern that makes it unique, rather like a fingerprint. For example, in very mundane terms a pad of paper bears the pattern of a rectangle with length, width, and height. One pad of paper will not match every other pad of paper in those three dimensions (or the binding used), but the basic structure is the same. Similarly, each human being has a body, blood, hair, fingernails, and so on, but the size, shape, color, scent, and personality shift within each to create uniqueness, a being we recognize as human but individual.

Relating this concept to a spiritual goal sounds difficult, but it really isn't. Just think of each goal as an energy vibration with its own characteristics. Love has a pattern. Peace and health have patterns. Prosperity, hope, and renewal have patterns. The tricky part is discerning the pattern, then knowing how to adapt it to more specific goals.

Perhaps we represent the pattern for happiness as a radiating sun with a heart in the middle (the sun often symbolizes joy and blessings while the heart is self). Now, go one step further and consider that you want to represent happiness between two people. Your basic symbolic value of "happiness" remains, but now there is more to consider than self. The imagery, which is also the pattern, might change to reflect this new goal by having two hearts joined in the center of the sun. While this example is only for illustrative purposes, it gives you a very good starting point for understanding and using the patterns of power to improve magickal manifestation.

Let's try another example. Picture a square, a pattern strongly associated with Earth energy. Now turn the square so it looks like a diamond and lay it over the first. You now have doubled the earthy nature of that pattern and created an eight-pointed star, which traditionally represents order and harmony. This makes perfect sense because Earth offers foundations. When you build positive energy on that foundation, you get structure! If you can begin to see magickal energy this way, you can pattern the energy raised from spells, rituals, prayers, and meditations similarly.

Activity 1.7 - Consider the Circle

A great deal of magick centers around circles. Why is that? Get some paper and a pen right now and think about the significance of the pattern we call "circle." What does that circle hold? What does it keep out? What is its central point? What does the border represent? Make a list of at least 20 words or phrases that come to mind about this simple symbol.

Now read the list. Can you narrow down your phrases and ideas to 10 or even five core concepts? If so, you're getting very close to discerning the circle's magickal energy pattern. Keep those core concepts handy, then draw a circle with a square around it. What happens to the energy when you square the circle? How do the two patterns enhance or engage each other? What would you personally use this symbol for if you were to apply it magickally?

You can change the basic patterns in this exercise to any geometric figure, gliff, sigil, or other sacred pattern you wish. Each time, follow the process of first honing your understanding of that pattern, then adding another motif to it. Keep diligent notes of what you discover in this process, as I can promise you will find them helpful in enchanted living.

By the way, it's often helpful to work with just one pattern (a simple one) at first for at least six months when trying to wrap your hands around this whole concept. Integrate it into various magickal methods whenever possible, taking care that it's the *right* pattern for the goal. Also:

* Recognize that pattern in nature when you see it. Where does it manifest? What does that tell you about that pattern's energy?

* Meditate on the pattern. How does it make you feel when you're done visualizing it laying over various chakra points, or when you see yourself inside that pattern? How does your aura feel afterward?

* Dance or move through the pattern to understand its physical presence. We do this every time we dance in a circle around a sacred fire; you're just taking it one step further. If you can, position your body like the pattern; sufis were known to do this to make them part of a greater universal motif.

* Express the pattern in an art and find ways of connecting with it sensually.

All the while, take notes of your experience. The time will be well spent. In the end you will intimately know how, where, when, and why to use that pattern of energy in your spirit and in your life. Then go on and explore another!

Plan Your Magick

In the previous exercise, you'll notice I asked you to pay close attention to the existing pattern and how it is affected by a new one. This is in order to learn how to gently and sensitively add one to the other (and perhaps to many more). Why the caution? Well, what would happen if someone randomly changed your town's street layout? It would be chaotic. Without planning all hell would break loose, people would get lost, and others would collide. Magick is the same way. Without planning and a sound pattern, your energy can go astray and accomplish nothing, or manifest incorrectly.

One great illustration of energy gone awry came to me from a woman I met in Ohio. She and a friend had done a fertility spell together because she wanted to have a baby and was having trouble. Unfortunately, her friend got pregnant at an inopportune time instead. The problem here was that while the original pattern was recognized (e.g. physical infertility), it was only partially so. The spell had to be contrived for one *specific* person, not just enacted without direction, so the energy pattern attached itself in the wrong place! This type of error is more common than any of us would like to admit.

Each human has a certain limit to their vision, both physically and metaphysically. We can predict, with some certainty, what the outcome of a particular action or spell might be on our present environment and the people in it. But what about all the people and things that environment and those individuals touch? At some point, we can see no further and must trust ourselves and our magick to take form for "the good of all." This also means taking care with our patterning so that, at least to the point where our spiritual event horizon begins, we know the energy has manifested for "the good of all."

This awareness also returns us full circle to living in the moment we're given. We seize the moment to fix whatever we may have done wrong and to learn from that mistake. We seize the moment to change our lives and the lives of those we love, to hold and heal the Earth. We seize the moment for magick!

Chapter 2

Sensual Sorcery: The Power of Five

"When you start using senses you've neglected, your reward is to see the world with completely fresh eyes."
—Barbara Sher

"Nothing can cure the soul but the senses, just as nothing can cure the senses but the soul."
—Oscar Wilde

While some things in everyday life are two dimensional (television is a good example), magick has the extra dimension of depth: a depth of feeling, experiencing, responsibility, awareness (in body, mind, and spirit), and ultimately, a depth of knowing. In this chapter, we will explore some metaphysical concepts and techniques that help us rediscover this depth and then activate it powerfully in our magick and our lives, starting with the power of five.

Now you might ask: What's in a number? Quite a lot actually. Numbers are an abstract that represent and communicate something concrete, just as in magick we use symbols to communicate what we hope to manifest. Pythagoras even went so far as to say that numbers are elements of all things.

Looking specifically at the number five as it appears in various ancient settings, we find that Celtic music was based in five tones. This configuration is also seen in Africa and Japan. Islam has five sacred duties that we'll discuss in detail in Part 2 of this book. The peace offering of the Israelites consisted of five lambs, goats, and rams.

In Rome, five represented love and commitment. In dream keys, the number five is said to portend uneasiness accompanied by change. And, last but not least, ancient magicians considered it a lucky number, quite possibly because we have five fingers, toes, and senses.

Speaking of magick and the senses, there are five points on the pentagram and five aspects to sacred space: Earth, Air, Fire, Water, and Spirit. Magick itself is a very sensual experience, bringing to bear (1) sights, (2) sounds, (3) smells, (4) tastes, and (5) touches to inspire the subconscious and superconscious self. So each of the five senses corresponds to a point on the pentagram and the circle: Sight is Fire, because we need illumination to see both physically and spiritually. Taste is Water; many old folk spells call for saliva as an empowering component. Touch is Earth; perhaps this is why we have touchstones and knock on wood! Smell is Air, which is linked to our vital breath, and hearing is Spirit: The difference between listening and hearing brings to bear the Spirit element.

With this in mind, it's easy to see why adding the senses into your spiritual processes would directly affect how detailed and specific your results will be. It is similar to putting together a puzzle. While you might be able to get a good idea of what the finished puzzle looks like without a few pieces in it, the details from one missing piece can change everything. Magick works similarly. Every sense you bring into your efforts is a part of the puzzle that provides greater dimension in the manifestation mechanism.

Here are some ways to consider bringing your senses directly into metaphysical processes.

Sight

Surround yourself with items that represent your goal before and during the effort. Don't forget about color symbolism here, as well as pieces of art and even everyday objects that visually inspire thoughts of what you hope to achieve, preferably in manifested form. If you can't find such an object, visualize something appropriate in the auditorium of your mind instead. Remember Practice 13 (page 17): In magick, a symbol is no less powerful than what it represents, be that symbol in the real world or the astral.

Sound

The presence and absence of sound both work. If, for example, you're trying to halt gossip, you probably will want a silent atmosphere, based on the law that like attracts like.

You can create sacred sounds yourself with chanting, mantras, songs, and affirmations, or put on a suitable recording with words, music, or sounds to help you achieve the right mental space. It's good if the musical piece also represents what you're trying to achieve. For example, gentle instrumentals aren't the best choice for building energy, but they are fantastic for gradual grounding or inspiring peace.

Taste

The phrase, "You are what you eat," says lots about how you use taste as a part of magick. When you consume suitable pre-ritual and spell foods, beverages, and even candies whose flavors linger, you internalize their associated energy. Then you can manifest that energy externally as you work. Some spiritual methods allow you to make foods or beverages part of the working (for example, including a libation). Others methods require a little more creativity, such as the idea of using hard candy chosen for its color or flavor symbolism in a communication spell. These can be kept in your mouth for quite a long time without interrupting things too much, unless, of course, you have to sing!

Touch

I am a very tactile person. The feel of an item can generate whole worlds of meaning for me, but even those people who are not so "touchy feely" can relate to the difference they feel between wearing something warm and fuzzy versus a business suit. These are the kinds of things to think about in adding the right textures into your methods. Let the feeling generated by the texture match the magickal theme.

Besides fabric and clothing, the texture of special objects, such as a tumbled crystal versus a faceted one, can help too. A smooth brass wand feels and responds very differently from a natural wooden one, for example.

Smell

Incense, anointing oils, perfumes, colognes, potpourri, flower arrangements, tinctures, and even air and carpet fresheners become the tools for this sense. If, for example, you're working a love spell in your home, clean the rug beforehand with a rose powder so that the smell and vibration remain to augment your work.

For portable magick, wear an aromatic that represents your active magickal goals so that energy penetrates directly into your aura and the areas that you frequent.

Activity 2.1 - Personalized Aromatics

For this activity, I ask you to consider which theme seems to influence your life the most when it comes to the various spiritual processes you enact (for example, love, health, peace, joy, power, protection, and prosperity). Now, go to your kitchen pantry and just smell some of the spices there. Do any make you think of this theme? If so, make a note of those aromatics (and just for the fun of it, check out that herb's metaphysical correspondences to see if those match!).

If you can't find something that makes your higher self say, "Aha!" try going through some essential oils at a health food store to find what you need. Once you've gathered the aromatics, steep or add them to a good oil base until you like the strength of the scent. Charge this oil by moonlight for intuitive/feminine themes, or sunlight for conscious/masculine themes. Store in an airtight container and dab on your chakra and pulse points whenever you want to activate that energy quickly and effectively.

Sound simple? It is! Practice 14 (page 17) for enchanted living states that things don't have to be complicated to work! Don't get caught up in the mundane mind-set that says "more = better"; spirituality doesn't work that way. In fact, many times simplicity evokes more power because you can give all your attention to the goal instead of the process (for example, the "why" instead of the "how").

Combine Sensory and Symbolic Input

Along the same lines, both simplicity and complexity will matter little if meaning gets lost. Practice 15 (page 17) says that meaning is everything. Even if you can't think of a good, meaningful way to incorporate all your senses into your magick, at least include those methods and senses that you relate to most strongly. Having those cues stimulating and supporting the magick similarly stimulates and supports results.

It's kind of neat to realize that putting all this sensory and symbolic input together creates a pattern, and in enchanted living Practice 22 (page 17) is that patterns equal power, realization, and manifestation (see also Chapter 1). So besides some of the examples already discussed, how exactly do we go about applying the power and pattern of five in our daily spiritual practices? It's actually not as difficult as you might think.

Activity 2.2 - Sacred Space

Set up your living space in such a way that it honors the power of five. Begin by picking out appropriate symbolic objects for the four quarter points and one for Spirit. Bless and energize these in a manner suited to your Path, then place them near the quarter and center points, perhaps under a rug or on a table. What does this accomplish? Each time you see those items, you're reminded of what they represent. This venerates those energies and makes them welcome in your home. This fulfills Practice 16 (page 17) for enchanted living: Always make room for Spirit and soul-fullness in your home and life. It does make a difference. An additional benefit here is that these objects set up an inactive sacred space in and around your home. So long as you honor that, you can call those energies into action any time you have a need.

Encourage Energy Flow

Physical positions provide you with another option for representing the five powers. Yogis do this regularly, positioning themselves in such a way as to be more receptive to the universe and encourage a free flow of energy. Similarly, the whirling dervishes spin themselves to make their body the center of the sacred space, the point of the mandala to, to unite with the Sacred.

Putting this into a more viable example for everyday folk, sitting or lying on the ground, for example, is a very earth-touch position. Standing with your arms raised might be an Air/smell position; hands to your ears could be a Spirit/hearing posture. Similarly, hands above your eyes is a Fire/sight position, and an open mouth could be a Water/taste position. If you can put yourself into direct contact with the appropriate Element at the same time, all the better.

It amazes me how many times people forget about the most important tool they have with them all the time: themselves! Practice 17 (page 17) for enchanted living is that our lives are the act of worship; we are the magick, and everything else is simply icing on the cake. The Sacred really doesn't care about our tools or clothing; those items are intended to get us past ourselves so we can focus on the mystical. Nonetheless, in the quest for enchanted living and the desire to become more spiritually adept, we have to be ready to accept the power within us.

With this in mind, I'd like to take a closer look at the value and function of the senses as a viable physical, readily available tool for our ongoing spiritual growth.

SEEING IS BELIEVING

> *"What is art but a way of seeing?"*
> —Thomas Berger

Think about how much reality is shaped by what you see. We often say, "Seeing is believing." This indicates a strong tie between vision and faith: If we can see something, we can believe it is possible. Metaphysically speaking, without faith, confidence, trust, and conviction, action becomes nothing more than rote dogma! This faith, however, needs to be based on something we can comprehend, something substantial (per Practice 15).

To give you a good example of how this works, we can look to an old form of visual spellcraft. The ancient Gnostics wrote the magickal word *abracadabra* in the form of a slowly decreasing triangle. Now, what's interesting linguistically is that abracadabra means "diminish like the word!" In this manner, the Gnostic mages combined the meaning of language with a visual form for double the results!

abracadabra

abracadabr

abracada

abracad

abraca

abrac

abra

abr

ab

a

Put these two visual cues—the shape and the meaning—together and you have very powerful sympathetic magick to help banish sickness or other problems. Try this yourself with a word that represents something you'd like to deter, or turn the symbol upside down and build energy instead! There's nothing that says you can't get creative here; in fact, I advocate it!

Another good example from spellcraft comes in the way that various components were treated. The Grimoires of ancient times talked about burning or burying symbolic objects so they literally disappear from view as part of bindings and banishings. In other words, the final physical condition of components somehow relates to the material goals, like gently binding poppets together in a love spell or taping a torn heart back together to heal a broken heart. In all these examples, seeing the symbol taken away or transformed helps convey meaning to our superconscious, release the magick within, and direct our power more efficiently.

People with a knack for carving, sculpting, painting, drama, pantomime, sewing, and other visual arts and crafts have many options for using the sense of sight in neat ways. Want to attract prosperity? Paint pennies from heaven, slowly adding more and more coins each day. Looking for a house? Take some clay and slowly shape your ideal house in that mound throughout the time you're searching. Need more self-love? Hug yourself as part of a spell. To augment a glamoury for beauty, make a poppet representing yourself and adorn it in visually pleasing ways. The idea is to create an image of your desire as if it had already manifested. After all, seeing is believing and this belief supports your magick.

Activity 2.3 - Shape It Up!

Think of a goal that you presently have on your proverbial spiritual platter. Consider how you might represent that goal as completed in three dimensions, specifically through a clay medium. Once you've got that image in mind, get some self-hardening clay. Set aside some time over several days where you can work on the clay, keeping your goal in mind as you shape the image you're visualizing (carefully wrap the clay in food wrap in between sessions so it doesn't dry up). Bear in mind this doesn't have to be a great work of art; you're the only person who has to recognize what it represents. When you're finally done, let the clay harden; this also "firms up" the energy symbolically. Put this somewhere you can see it often, which also supports the energy visually, until manifestation. At that point, you can either ritually destroy the object or keep it as a wonderful reminder of the power of sight.

Visual Reminders Aid Magick

Many rituals also illustrate the power of sight. Ancient shamans often put on ritual masks and costumes because they felt this appeased and honored the spirits whom they supplicated. Equally important, for the other participants in the ritual, this transformed "good old Joe" into a formidable image: that of a god, goddess, or powerful spirit who could help with pressing needs. We still use masks and costumes in rituals because they visually remind us that this is a magickal/spiritual procedure, which symbolizes the purpose of the ritual to all those gathered.

For those not comfortable with the idea of wearing masks or costumes, try simpler, "user friendly" alternatives. For example, put on light, diaphanous, or pastel-colored clothing for your Spring rites. Change your clothes as part of a ritual for self-transformation, leaving the old "you" behind and literally donning the new one! Make sure to have a mirror handy! Try some creative body paints, face makeup, jewelry, hats, scarves, and so on. Remember, your visual cues need not be dramatic, only meaningful.

Beyond this, anything that you can put around you that keeps your mind on the task at hand and your thoughts centered on Spirit can be considered a "good thing." Practice 1 (page 17) for enchanted living states that without mental focus and fortitude in the tangible present, very little will happen metaphysically in the future.

The good news is that these decorative items need not make sense to anyone but you, unless you're working in a group. When you work in tandem with others, it's important to remain sensitive to more universal visual cues to which others can respond so you can all reach the same place together. A good book of symbolism might be helpful to this task. Two that I recommend are Barbara Walker's *Woman's Dictionary of Symbols and Sacred Objects* (Harper & Row, 1988) and Miranda Bruce-Mitford's *Illustrated Book of Signs and Symbols* (DK Publishing, 1996).

Simpler still is the visual cue we can create with our own bodies. Some priestesses raise their arms, guiding the cone of power on its way. Some practitioners cast a circle using the pointer finger to channel energy as opposed to a wand. Sitting on the ground at the end of a ritual helps us return to normal levels of awareness. Turning your hands outward directs the energy of a spell outward, and turning them inward directs that energy to you. These examples show how we can create physically meaningful postures from which we can see and feel the desired effect.

Activity 2.4 - Posturing

On a piece of paper, write each of these words on a separate line with about three lines between each: hands, feet, legs, arms, head. Now, next to each word, write down ways that you could alter the positioning of each of these so it reflects a goal and also influences your sense of vision. For example, simply turning your head in one direction or the other will change your view. Turning it to the right (clockwise) might correspond to building positive energy, while turning it to the left (counterclockwise) could augment banishing. Come up with as many different ideas as you can and keep them somewhere. Refer back to the list before you create a spell, ritual, meditation, or whatever to see which of these postures might be integrated to augment your goal. Make notes of the successes so you can use them again.

Visualization Improves Results

What about times when you can't have the best posturing or objects around for that visual input? Go to the theater of your mind and visualize! Here we create imagery that reflects our goals, heightens our level of awareness, integrates an idea or lesson, clarifies something, and improves perspectives. Your thoughts are very powerful, and while visualization might be considered a will-driven form of imagining, its potential for magick shouldn't be underestimated.

Zolar, a metaphysical writer of some acclaim, once said that the power to make and change the mind lies within. Visualization helps with that process while neatly fulfilling the visual part of the equation. Seeing with your spiritual eyes instead of outside with physical ones doesn't change anything. In fact, because the goal is to become the magick, visualization improves results, especially with psychic matters that require a keenly honed sense of inner vision!

Visualization has the additional benefit of releasing us from material constraints. Here, anything is possible, even if it might be impossible in the real world. For example, a visualization aimed at personal liberation could take the form of seeing yourself floating or flying without any external aid. So, when circumstances don't allow a lot of external imagery, or the need requires symbolic input that isn't likely on a temporal level, make what you need internally!

I find it interesting and very profound that we refer to eyes as "the windows of the soul." When we get creative about how we open this sensual window, it similarly opens the way for some marvelous, personalized magick. Practice 19 (page 17) for enchanted living is that you are your own best guru and guide, so personalizing magick isn't only fun, it's functional and necessary to progressing along the path toward true enlightenment with our eyes wide open!

AN EAR ON THINGS

"The mind is for seeing, the heart is for hearing."
—Saudi Arabian proverb

Each person has the ability to hone his/her senses, but some will experience more success with one sense than another. So, if after reading this chapter, you find that hearing (or any other sense) isn't as emotionally and mentally stimulating as another sense, don't be discouraged. This is quite natural. You can still work on developing spiritually centered hearing, but do it in conjunction with the sense that provides you more personal satisfaction and input. Practice 20 (page 17) for enchanted living states that you should improvise and practice, practice, practice!

Getting back to listening, sound is a wave of energy that has a pattern. This pattern has an astral presence that we can learn to "hear," even as a psychic "hears" spirits whispering. By training ourselves to hear in this unique way, we can tune into astral sound signatures, the patterns of which reveal a great deal about magick and life. The difficulties for most people are learning how to listen astrally and understanding what is heard.

The key to success spiritually is learning to listen on a mundane level first. There's a huge difference between just hearing and really listening. To illustrate, consider how many arguments erupt between people because of a discrepancy between what one thought they heard and what the other person really said or meant. This happens because each person listens differently, with personal bias, with cultural bias, and with the bias of distraction. As we acquire the ability to hear from a more universal standpoint, a great deal of bias can be filtered out. We can instead tune into more universal symbols that we hear with spiritual ears.

Activity 2.5 - Just Listen

For this activity, I want you to take a whole day to yourself and dedicate it to your sense of listening. Throughout this day, carry a pad and paper with you and make notes of the impressions and information you gather. Say nothing; assume nothing. Just listen.

At first, listen with the ears that tune into the world as a whole. Next, narrow that focus and listen to one conversation from both perspectives. Third, listen to the auric presence of one person. What do you hear there? Finally, stop for a minute and hear everything that's going on around you. Filter external sounds out and turn your focus inward. Hear only your breath and the beating of your heart. Do you find you feel different? Does the clamor from the world around you seem less important than it did just a few moments ago? Make notes of your experiences with listening on various levels and then compare them to what you read in the rest of this section.

Enhance Interpersonal Communication

Selective spiritual hearing is very helpful to interpersonal communications. Really open your ears when you're with others, focusing on not just what they're saying and doing, but also on the sounds that vibrate all around them. What type of music does a person's aura create? Is there harmony? Remember, astral static may not mean this person is bad or dishonest. It could simply mean that you and he/she are not on the same figurative channel, like a cosmic radio where each person is on a specific frequency. When you tune into that frequency, what you hear is symbolic of how positive or negative that person/situation will likely be for you.

To put this into context, let's say you've been searching for a coven in which to participate. You go to one gathering and quietly "listen" to the proceedings. If the astral sounds you pick up on are consonant and blend well with your own, you can be fairly confident that you've found a potential home. Conversely, if the astral music you hear seems dissonant, haphazard, or just "off" somehow, your spiritual ears may be telling you something important. Perhaps the group is going through a restructuring period that's causing confusion. Perhaps the group has some internal strife. Maybe the members are just having an "off" magickal night (hey, it happens to the best of us). Perhaps the universe is gently saying no about this particular group for you.

Interpreting Sounds

How do we interpret the sounds that come through? It's very personal. Your mind will interpret the unseen world in symbols that make sense to you. So if you associate the sound of bells with joy and you hear bells in a person's aura, it would stand to reason that you've met a happy person! Don't overlook those first gut-instinct interpretations that come to you. They're often right! And for those sounds with which you don't have an immediate experiential or intuitive response, use this general reference as a guide:

* Static: Possible deception; someone on a completely different wavelength with whom you'll likely have trouble communicating.
* Harmonious: Peace with self; someone with whom you'll likely communicate effectively.
* Singular: An independent, very focused nature that may have trouble seeing viewpoints outside its own.
* Erratic: Someone uncertain of his/her direction or who vacillates a lot depending on the proverbial "wind" that's blowing.
* Dull: Someone who is not overly exciting but very predictable.
* Pulsing: Intense energy that can augment or disrupt, depending on how it's applied.
* Flowing: Positive energy, often transformational or healing, that can work well with almost anyone because of a flexible nature.
* Dissonant: Someone who is not whole in self, and who may actually have a harmful agenda.

Bear in mind that the loudness of each of these bits of input changes their value slightly (similar to a volume control).

Bringing Meaningful Sounds to Rituals

Let's apply this whole concept of spiritual hearing in the arena of spells, rituals, and other magickal methods. As with touch and sight, adding hearing into any metaphysical technique should improve the outcome because of the extra dimension the sensual cue provides. We have been taught from childhood to quickly react to sounds like a honking horn or our mother's voice in warning. This can prove very useful for empowering our magick because of the immediate conscious and subconscious energy that our response provides!

Thanks to the wonders of technology, one need not be overly talented to bring meaningful sounds into rituals. Put on some symbolically appropriate music, then listen and uplift your spirit! Open your spiritual ears to each person working the ritual with you so you know when he/she is ready to help direct the cone of power, or when he/she should perhaps sit things out due to weariness, anger, or sickness. Listen closely to each group member's breathing and match your breath with everyone else's to create harmony. Listen to the static in the room that comes when magick is happening! These sounds from your spiritual ears assure you that you're weaving your rituals effectively.

The spiritual drummer's art is heavily dependent on hearing the other drummers and what the spirit of the drum is saying. There are four voices here: the drum, the musician, Spirit and the harmony of everyone working together. Truly attuned drummers can use the power of this tool to transform the atmosphere of a ritual for the good of all. But this happens only when the drummers really listen, and when those gathered hear the drum's voice speaking through their spiritual ears.

In talking about percussion, don't overlook the sounds you can make with your body including chanting, mantras, clapping, stomping, and finger snapping. Chanting and clapping are especially good for raising power because you can increase the volume or speed as the magick grows. The effect these sounds will have depends on listening keenly to them and allowing the magickal pattern to fill you to overflowing.

Stomping and finger snapping have some interesting applications for spellcraft. When one hears a stomping sound, the natural tendency is to think of overcoming, figuratively stomping out a problem. So, use a stomping sound to signal the release of your magick in a victory spell. Again, remember that the volume of the sound does affect the results. Finger snapping might be added to a spell where you need something to manifest quickly and easily. Snap at an appropriate moment to help direct the magick at just the right time.

Beyond this, every theme of every metaphysical working creates a sound all its own. When you hear dissonance at the end of a working, it's highly likely that something has gone awry. If, on the other hand, you hear a melodious sound as you close a ritual, that note in your mind cues the release and direction of energy and provides assurance that you've completed the task effectively.

Use Your Inner Sense of Hearing

Now, I'll admit that there are some circumstances that don't lend themselves to verbalizations, music, and other sounds. When this happens, don't forget that thoughts are words uttered inwardly. At times when making noise is not appropriate because of our surroundings, we can use our inner sense of hearing to manifest results. Think your sounds!

Or, for another marvelously subtle approach, try humming a magickal ditty to improve your mood. Most people think nothing of a little humming, and only you will know the significance of the tune! As you hear that music and think of all it represents, it can help you carry your magick wherever you may be with little difficulty.

Sounds Heighten Awareness

Two other sounds that affect spiritual seekers deeply are those of our body's breath and heartbeat. Paying close attention to one or both of these often improves meditative states. An additional benefit here is that many of us remain unaware of our body's signals. By listening to the rhythm of our breathing or heartbeat we can learn to calm ourselves, center, and create symmetry among body, mind, and spirit.

A variety of other sounds have been used in meditation methods to improve focus and heighten awareness. These include the sound of a bell or gong, that of voices raised in "Om," or quiet New Age music. I like a bell or gong because the gentle after-sounds seem vibrationally helpful to centering and deepening the meditative state. If you wish, add a little visualization so you "see" the sound as light that settles into the center of your being.

Activity 2.6 - Combining Sight and Sound

For this activity, sit comfortably with your back straight, in a chair or on the floor. Take three deep cleansing breaths and clear out any mundane thoughts. Focus wholly on your intention to marry vision and sound into a harmonious whole. At this juncture begin chanting, singing, or praying, all the while maintaining your meditative focus. Continue like this for at least five minutes until the chant, song, or prayer is moving of its own accord (meaning it feels natural not forced).

Next, begin to imagine the sounds that you're making like a beacon of light pouring down from above you. What color is that light? What shapes does it create above and around you? You are discovering the pattern of power in that chant, song, or prayer! Better still, you can visualize how that pattern interacts with that of your own spirit for transformational results. Make sure to make notes of what you experienced in this activity; by the way, you may find that other senses want to get into the show too (for example, smelling the pattern or picking up a textural appeal).

I cannot overstress the need we have in our community for truly honed spiritual ears. There are many people in need who have trouble voicing that need. Spiritual ears can hear the words these people cannot say. Likewise, listening with the ears of Spirit can avoid a lot of misunderstandings that arise from rushed or ill-considered conversation. The harmony and unity of our community is vital, so keep one ear to the ground, and the other to the Goddess.

MAGICK IS IN THE AIR

"Behave so the aroma of your actions may enhance the general sweetness of the atmosphere."
—Henry David Thoreau

The nose comes up in conversation all the time. We "keep our noses to the grindstone." We "nose into" other people's business. Some folks have a "nose" for a windfall or disaster. What do these phrases tell us about our sense of smell on a spiritual level? Perhaps most importantly, it shows us that aromas affect our perceptions and focus, both of which are very important to effective spiritual pursuits.

Similar to any other sense, each aroma in the world has an astral presence that accompanies it. Additionally, these evoke memories, emotions, and other reactions, the energy of which can be used to excite your magick. For example, I find the smell of cookies in the oven incredibly tantalizing, and it usually lifts my spirits. The smell of bread brings back memories of my grandmother, whose food was always filled with love, so much so you could taste it. So, if I can smell some fresh-baked bread during a love spell or ritual, it automatically brings up that emotion, which I can then pour into my magick. Because of this intimate way in which aroma affects people, you can easily see where pantry enchantments are enhanced considerably by choosing foods, beverages, and other components according to the feelings their aromas create!

Activity 2.7 - Personal Aromatherapy Kit

This activity builds on Activity 2.1, and you can take what you learned there and use it as a starting point. To know which scents affect you, and how they affect you, the first step is simply experimenting. Take an item with a specific aroma into a relatively bland environment. Just as it's hard to choose a perfume or cologne at a shop's counter because so many other scents surround the one you're testing, it's also hard to ascertain the spiritual and metaphysical significance of various aromas when a lot of other smells fill the air.

Next, take three deep cleansing breaths before actually smelling the item. If it has a particularly strong aroma, don't put it right up to your nose. Remember, the true power of a scent isn't in how "strong" it is, but in its vibrations and how they affect you. Sit back and let that aroma settle into your spirit. Make mental notes of any visual images, memories, feelings, colors, or other responses you get, and write them down when you're done.

Over time you'll create an extensive list of scents and the meaning of each for you. In effect, you've just designed your own system of aromatherapy! Continue this way with other items in and around your home, which also happen to bear your energy signature.

Choosing Aromatics Purposefully

As early as 1500 B.C., healers were using aromatics like lavender as part of curatives. Egyptians often used aromatherapy to treat depression, while Babylonians perfumed the temples to please the Divine. Even Hippocrates advocated various scents as being healthy. So, why can't we likewise use our sense of smell to improve the "health" of our magick?

Actually, we probably *have* been doing this all along without necessarily knowing it. For example, sage has an emotional and physical "cleansing" ability, and we use it in ritual circles to purify the sacred space. Also, many practitioners use incense as a meditative tool. The main difference now will be choosing our aromatics a little more purposefully.

For example, one might add a specific aroma to a spell to cooperate with and support the energy, as well as providing that all important sensual cue. To illustrate, say that when you experiment with the scent of fresh oranges you discover you associate their aroma with healing. The next time you are performing a spell for personal vitality, you could design it around this fruit as a component. In this instance you might add an incantation:

> *The scent of orange upon the winds,*
> *So the magick may begin*
> *And on that wind, the aroma charged by design*
> *By my will, good health be mine!*

As you say the word *wind,* light incense. And, at the end of the spell, add another sense into the equation by drinking some orange juice!

With charms and amulets, add specific aromatics to your bundles so that the energy of that scent goes with you everywhere. The important thing in this case is to make sure any aromatically charged charm or amulet's smell stays fresh. When the scent dissipates, so does the magick. To refresh the scent, try dabbing some essential oil on the charm or amulet; putting in new, blessed herbs; and/or adding orris root to the components when it's first prepared to help "fix" the scent.

Aromatics in Ritual

These types of aromatic gestures translate perfectly well into the ritual environment too. Put elementally aligned aromatics at the four quarter points, burn an incense that honors your deity, or put some fresh flowers on the altar so their scent lightly touches the air in Spring. Just make sure you remember to bring what you need into the sacred space!

Don't be afraid to experiment to bring this sense to life; it will make every breath a uniquely spiritual and magickal experience. Take a long walk in the woods and notice the shifting scents and energies that speak of the Mother. Or, stride through your home and sniff at the air; what answers lie there for you about what's been happening in the house lately? You'll find that the nose really does know!

Magick is truly in the Air, and the Goddess is afoot. When we learn to recognize the subtle lessons of our senses we cannot help but grow in body, mind, and spirit.

A MATTER OF TASTE

*"Create, and be true to yourself, and depend only
on your own good taste."*
—Duke Ellington

Every flavor we experience evokes memories, emotions, and other reactions, the energy of which can be used to excite your magick. For example, I find that the taste of warm bread evokes a kind of centering and peace that's wonderful after a ritual. It helps ground me, but doesn't erase the sense of lingering energy in my aura. Combine that with the aroma, and the emotional result is quite profound!

To know which flavors affect you in different ways, the first step is simply experimenting as you did with aromatics. Start keeping a food and beverage notebook. Close your eyes when you eat, and let the flavors linger on your taste buds. What thoughts come to mind when you do this? What kind of feelings do you get on the edge of your awareness? Trust your instincts here; they won't betray you. Write down whatever comes to mind and refer back to those correspondences whenever you wish.

I personally find that the taste of roast beef rekindles my maternal instincts because it's a food my mother always made for us on special occasions. To this day, I can't eat a roast without sensing the special magick of motherhood close by. So, when I, as a mother, feel a little less than "on," I might nibble some roast beef, internalize that flavorful memory, and allow it to manifest within and without.

You can do similarly. This illustration is actually a very simple kind of sympathetic magick that relies heavily on personal experience and how you feel about what you're tasting. As with all your other senses, the personal factor is an absolute guidepost to other spiritual applications, and of course it helps if you actually like what you're tasting! It makes internalization much easier. I've found that "taste" magick doesn't work very well if you find yourself scrunching up your face with horror at the flavor, unless you happen to be trying to banish something!

Activity 2.8 - Taste the Wind

We often get into the habit of thinking of our senses on a very flat level. We smell flowers or perfume, but how many of us stop to smell the wind, or the sunshine, or the leaves after a rain storm. Each of these scents can hold words of meaning from nature's classroom, when we stop long enough to really pay attention.

With this in mind, take a couple of hours someday to smell things of which you wouldn't normally think. Start with this book! Pick it up. Center yourself, and gently furl the pages about four inches from your mouth. Take a deep breath through your mouth. What kind of taste does the paper put into the air? How does the book taste mystically? Make notes of your experience with this experiment so you can refer to them in trying other unusual items.

Edible Magick

So, how do we apply this concept in spellcraft, charms, and rituals? For one, I think this could be a wonderful dimension to add to charm and amulet creation. Dried foods, candy, and anything else that is edible and easily portable is perfect for magick that you can literally take with you anywhere. Returning to my roast beef example, I might substitute some beef jerky and carry it in my purse for those public moments when children inevitably want mommy in her most sublime form! Or, if I want to sweeten my disposition and the way I communicate with them, I might follow it with a mint!

Mind you, I can't just nibble on these things idly without intention and expect that magick will happen. Practice 21 (page 17) for enchanted living is to always work with intention. To highlight that intention, we can turn to all our other magickal techniques: visualization, incantations, prayer, and/or focus. Visualize a suitable color of light energy being released from the food or beverage while you consume it, spreading with the flavor throughout your body. Incant a verse that directs your intention into the item just before you consume it. Finally, eat or drink very slowly, allowing the full flavor of the item to remain on your senses so that the pattern of energy it creates extends into what you're trying to accomplish.

Build Supportive Energy with Flavor

In spellcraft, try using flavor to manifest specific emotional or physical responses at important points in a spell.

This will help you build more supportive energy. For example, if your experiments with an apple yield the result that you associate this flavor with wellness, then the next time you're performing a spell for personal well-being, you could design it around this fruit as a component. In this instance, you might have an incantation such as:

When through my lips, this apple passes,
health and well-being lasts.
when it's flavor dances on my tongue,
by my will, this spell's begun!

It's a good idea to touch the apple to your tongue when you say the word *tongue* and then eat a piece at the end of the spell.

Let's try another illustration using a beverage for a similar goal. Instead of a whole apple, an obvious liquid alternative here would be some apple juice or cider. Now we change the incantation to mirror the change of venue:

I drink of the apple, whose health shall shine
throughout this beverage, golden and fine.
I accept the energy of this nectar pure,
the taste of apples, my health insures!

Now drink down the whole glass of juice, allowing its energy to tantalize your taste buds and fill every cell of your body through the digestion process.

Flavorful Rituals

These types of gestures translate perfectly well into the ritual environment, too. Similarly, I think you could easily use flavors to awaken your senses as part of the preparation for meditation. You can accomplish two things at once by using this as an opportunity to ponder your reactions to a specific taste as well. For example, I associate the flavor of tea with meditation because it seems to help still my busy mind and calm my body to a place where meditation is easier. So, I might have a nice cup of my favorite tea before meditating as step one.

Step two would be taking a variety of teas with me to my meditation space. After reaching a heightened state of awareness, I could then go through each tea and thoughtfully consider its potential in my spiritual life and magick, making notes of the results for future reference. I might later compare these to my initial reactions from the food and beverage experiments mentioned earlier in this chapter.

The wonderful thing about this whole idea is that it really is a matter of personal taste as to how you apply it and what you use to activate that special energy. Don't be afraid to experiment to bring this sense to life; it will make every meal and every snack into a potentially powerful experience filled with magick.

KEEPING IN TOUCH

> *"If you can learn from hard knocks, you can also learn from soft touches."*
> —Carolyn Kenmore

Think about sayings such as "reach out and touch someone"; "that person's awfully touchy"; "s/he is a touchy-feely type"; and so forth. These give us some awareness of how important touch is to human nature. Science has gone one step further and shown that gentle touching is essential to normal emotional and mental development in young animals. By extension, bringing the element of touch into our spells, rituals, and other methods will help us inspire healthy spiritual development.

Better still, touch (often communicated through textures) not only has an astral imprint but also a pattern. This means that when used properly, texture helps literally weave our spells into an astral form that feels three dimensional to our superconscious. It will also have a unique quality, one that combines the individual energy signature with the textural pattern that we can sense. This in turn fulfills Practice 22 (page 17): Patterns equal power, realization, and manifestation when treated respectfully and applied sensitively.

With this in mind, I like to incorporate touch into my personal rituals by choosing symbolic items that feel like their respective Elements. The presence of the appropriate texture honors the Element I'm calling. For example, I might leave a damp cloth or cup filled with water at the western quarter of the magick circle and touch it when I invoke that watchtower, which also neatly honors that elemental power. Some other good textural cues for the Elements include warm sand or a lit candle for Fire (be careful not to burn yourself); soil or a leaf for Earth; and smoke from incense or perhaps a fan, for Air. For those wishing to commune with elemental spirits, having textural cues is vital to the success of your endeavor.

What about the clothing you wear? Does the feel of the fabric moving against your skin change your attitude in subtle ways? If you're not sure, test drive the idea using the following activity:

Activity 2.9 - Seasonal Textures

For a Spring ritual, layer a heavy winter robe over successive layers of other clothing, the one closest to your skin being a lightweight, chiffon-like robe or shirt. Slowly remove the layers so that by the time you've raised a cone of power, only the diaphanous fabric remains to celebrate the liberating, airy nature of the season. Note whether the change in the weight and sensations created by the fabric improved the experience for you. If so, definitely make tactile considerations when choosing ritual garb! And, by the way, you can reverse this process come Winter.

The Important Sense of Touch

Textural cues don't end there, however. Textures have great value in spellcraft. For example, if you want to offer comfort to someone, surround his or her picture with cotton balls. Or, if you want to create a strong auric barrier around yourself, you might surround your own picture with tough materials like wood.

During meditation, a heightened sense of touch can dramatically improve interpersonal communications similar to hearing. When you find yourself at the stage where the outer edges of your aura feel slightly fuzzy, extend your psychic sense of touch to someone else's aura. How does their aura feel? Is it sticky, itchy, smooth, soft? Your interpretation of this sensation will provide you insights into that person's demeanor and intentions. For example, the sticky person might be somewhat dishonest or clingy, where a smooth aura could indicate someone with whom you could have similarly smooth interactions.

Also, I've found the textures in my clothing can make a huge difference in how well a meditation goes. If a shirt tag is constantly scratching at my neck, the effort won't likely be successful. On the other hand, if I'm in comfortable attire that makes me feel special and magickal, it's likely to improve the meditative state. In this case, clothes really do make the person!

Visualization gives you an opportunity to combine two senses for improved spiritual results. For example, visualize your aura having the nap and weave of flannel to create an aura of casual friendliness. Or, create a textured weave to change the shape of your aura so it will conform better to situational constraints.

I find it enlightening that we use the phrase, "keeping in touch," to describe the networks in our lives. In times when rediscovering and reaching out to our respective "tribes" is becoming more and more important, touch is there to help us. Even beyond those we consider friends and family, when you see a fellow human being in need, find a way to touch their lives. Sometimes this touch can be physical, sometimes it's mental, and sometimes it's magickal, but in any case it's a blessing to share. It will make the world a better place in which to live.

Building on the Basics

I realize some of you reading this may be saying, "Hey, this stuff is pretty elementary." Yes, it is. But like any good lesson plan, one needs to begin with the basics, then build on them. Without a sound understanding of the senses and how they affect spiritual pursuits, it is very difficult to move forward on your Path. Without an understanding of how to apply those senses metaphysically, you won't get the kinds of results desired from enchanted living. If, however, you apply these foundational tidbits creatively to the following four archetypes, then you can also anticipate some amazing changes, and some amazing magick.

Part 2:

The Way, the Path: The Ends and Means

"First, have a definite, clear practical ideal; a goal, an objective. Second, have the necessary means to achieve your ends: wisdom, money, materials, and methods. Third, adjust all your means to that end."

—Aristotle

"Without a quest, life is quickly reduced to bleak black and wimpy white, a diet too bland to get anybody out of bed in the morning. A quest fuels our fire. It refuses to let us drift downstream gathering debris."

—Charles Swindoll

Chapter 3

The Tao of Enchanted Living

"Truth's like a fire, and will burn through and be seen."

—Maxwell Anderson

The word *Tao* means quite simply "the way." It's amazing that two little words could mean so much. In Taoist tradition, this "way" or path cannot be defined; it must simply be experienced. Tao, by definition, also embodies the energy that is around and within all things, nourishing the universe with symmetry. So, the way back to the Divine and to spiritual balance and maturity is already readily accessible. All we need do is recognize, activate, and illustrate that truth in our everyday life.

How? That's where Part II of this book comes into play. What I'm introducing here is one technique for realizing the goal of enchanted living. I've found this system highly successful. Nonetheless, because you are not I, please remember to bring your vision and voice, your life's experiences and magickal awareness, to this foundation. With a sound construct, creativity, and honest effort working together, all that remains is waiting to then see how the Tao flowers within and without (per Practice 15, page 17).

Chapters 4 through 7 present various ideas, philosophies, theories, and applications based on four shamanic archetypes: Healer, Teacher, Warrior, and Visionary. Each of these archetypes can be a Path unto itself, or part of a greater whole— the wheel of your life. I personally feel that a spiritual seeker truly living the magick will eventually round out the corners of his or her life with all four!

FOUR ARCHETYPES ILLUSTRATE THE CIRCLE OF LIFE

Why use these particular archetypes? Because they are among the most consistently seen in many spiritual settings, and because they illustrate the Circle of Life in such a wonderful way. Think about it for a minute. If you are not whole, you can't truly understand wholeness, nor can you reach out to others and give fully (Healer). If you can't reach out to others and share thorough knowledge, you cannot instruct with honor (Teacher). That's one half of the Circle.

Continuing around, if you cannot teach honorably, you cannot defend the greater truths for the good of all because you, yourself, aren't completely aware or living them as yet (Warrior). And if you cannot defend truth, you certainly can't seek out a new vision that will create wholeness (Visionary). This takes us back to the top of the wheel to Healer.

Now, before that sounds too lofty or difficult an undertaking, it's a given that achieving perfection in any of these stages is not a simple task. In fact, you may find that you activate your Inner Healer, Teacher, Warrior, and Visionary on one level only to realize there is yet another horizon ahead. That's perfectly normal because the wheel keeps moving!

As you awaken these special aspects of self, you can only develop them to the spiritual level within which you presently live, not where you'll be a year from now. As you do, those archetypes will transform you from inside out. So, by the time you've gone through the entire wheel and are back to Healer, it will also be time to begin again as a "new" you!

Applying the Archetypes

In exploring each one of the four Paths, various beliefs and activities are provided to help you better understand and activate that archetype in your life on a very personal and profound level. To accomplish this in an orderly manner, each archetype is set up with seven subheadings. The following list explains these subheadings for your reference:

* **Keynote**: If you think of a keynote as the underlying melody of a very complex piece of music, you will be on the right track. The keynote of an archetype focuses the purpose and perspective of that archetype on a few key words or phrases that will help you unlock the meaning of that archetype on a personal level.

* **Shamanic Focus**: Shamanism is very pragmatic and down to earth. The Shamanic focus of an archetype brings everything home to where you live. It asks you to consider how this archetype may affect your thoughts and actions, not just metaphysically but also in the "real" world.

* **The Eight-Fold Path (Buddhism) Spotlight**: The Eight-Fold Path of Buddhism aims toward perfecting every corner of our reality. It does not do this with lofty words, but by encouraging openness. Each focus on the Eight-Fold Path is like water to the seed of your spirit and soul.

By remaining open to its lesson, that seed naturally grows into joy, peace, and wisdom. The eight segments of this path are defined as having (or working toward) right and proper views, thought, speech, action, livelihood, diligence, mindfulness, and concentration. Two of these will be explored in each of the four chapters that follow.

* **Sensory Cue**: In Chapter 2, we examined the importance of the five senses as readily available tools that we can hone and apply for our spiritual well-being. Now we'll take that idea one step further and show how an archetype applies one of the senses for improved expression of its lessons and powers.

* **Magickal Methods**: Meditation, visualization, projection, discipline, repatterning, self-empowerment, ritual, sacred journeys, and manifestation are all things discussed in a variety of magickal settings. As with the Eight-Fold Path, each of these aligns itself nicely with one of the four archetypes, actualizing that energy and giving it greater expression.

* **Elemental Correspondence**: Earth, Air, Fire, and Water: These are the building blocks of creation. Any symbol so strongly illustrated in nature's book is one to which we should pay attention. In my opinion, the Elements constitute a divine blueprint of sorts, the patterns from which are foundational to many mystical studies and methods. Thus, one of the four Elements will be discussed in each chapter that follows along with its function or value to the archetype in question.

* **Sacred Duty (Islam):** The Pillars of Islam require that every devotee undertake sacred duties, among them being regular cleansing, going on a pilgrimage, making offerings, and reciting prayers. With a little respectful adaptation, all of these pillars have tremendous value to enchanted living, and again each corresponds to an archetype nicely!

At the beginning of each one of the subheads in a chapter, I suggest that you stop momentarily and think carefully about the journey you're undertaking. This isn't something to jump into blindly. What you do with this information is going to affect everything in your life and the lives of those around you. Are you ready to make a commitment to yourself and Spirit to see the process through? Are you ready to welcome and honor those transformations? It won't always be easy, but it is well worth it!

By the way, it's perfectly normal to experience setbacks and failures along the way. Beyond such experiences being great teachers and keeping us humble, no one masters spiritual principles over night. In fact, few of us master them in one lifetime! With this in mind, please take these archetypes at your own pace (per Practice 6, page 16), anticipating at least three months, and possibly years, to reach a level of proficiency in any one of these (let alone all four!).

Knowing and honoring yourself means that you realize Practice 23 (page 17) already. Spirituality is not about keeping up with someone else whom you perceive as adept. No matter how talented or wise that person may seem, he/she is just as human as you are. The only real gauge you need to judge your growth lies on the altar of your heart. As long as you listen to and trust that voice within, you will rarely go astray.

Chapter 4

The Healer

> *"The concept of total wellness recognizes that our every thought, word, and behavior affects our greater health and well-being. And we, in turn, are affected not only emotionally but also physically and spiritually."*
> — Greg Anderson

Healer heal thyself. We hear this aphorism often. Such old sayings become "old sayings" because of some level of truth they bear. In this instance, the truth we glean is that one of the most sacred duties of any spiritual seeker is first to heal himself or herself from inside out. We cannot honestly reach out beyond ourselves and give fully when we ourselves are not whole. Now, having said that, it is quite true that akin to the quest for enlightenment, healing is also a lifelong journey. So how do you begin, and how do you know when you are ready to tap into the Inner Healer and release that power in your daily reality? This is no small question, but it is one that this chapter hopes to answer.

Before moving into that framework, however, let me share one of the most important lessons in this book: namely, healing recognizes love as a powerful ally (as does magick). Healers are the world's greatest lovers because you must love something to make it whole. Healers soften the hard heart;

they open energy blockages. This means loving, softening, and opening yourself, too. Practice 24 (page 17) in enchanted living is to not expect anyone else to accept or do something that you, yourself, are not willing to accept or do. It's a point of integrity.

Spiritual healing requires a cooperative effort between healer, patient, and Spirit (even when you are both the Healer and the patient!). The concept of reciprocity calls the Healer to receive as well as give, in willingness. Without that trinity, without that willingness, the results falter and fall flat. Why begin this archetype with that limitation? Because honoring, believing in, knowing, and loving one's self requires nothing less.

You should discard any preconceived notions you may have about what constitutes healing. Some of the smallest gestures of which you might not even think can heal: the touch of a hand, the warmth of a smile, the laughter of children. Healing is not about flash and fanfare; it's about little marvels that lift our burdens, make life more joyful and loving, and help us hold an image of wholeness in our heart and minds like the treasure it is.

KEYNOTE: AWARENESS

"Whatever we are waiting for—peace of mind, contentment, grace, the inner awareness of simple abundance—it will surely come to us, but only when we are ready to receive it with an open and grateful heart."

—Sarah Ban Breathnach

The Healer within strives to be completely aware of self, others, society, Earth, and far beyond that realm. As a person claims that awareness, he/she also holds tight to the gift of wholeness, seeing it as a pattern that exhibits itself throughout the universe. The cycle of life, death, and rebirth has closure and wholeness. Galaxies move in circles around a central point becoming a mandala of wholeness, the Circle. Even though this symbolism is around us all the time, to appreciate that pattern and apply it requires awareness.

Awareness, in the broadest sense, is a constant state of readiness. It means being attentive to the moment in which one lives and giving yourself fully to it (per Practice 1, page 16). It also means being aware of the moments that came before this one, and those that are just around the corner. In this manner, body, mind, and spirit become attuned to past, present, and future in a very powerful way.

Each person is a sum of his or her experiences. To truly know someone, to be wholly aware of them, you have to have at least some level of perception of his or her experiences and how they've shaped that individual. If you don't think this is true, just watch what happens the next time you mention a "sensitive" subject to someone because you didn't know it was sensitive!

Similarly, to achieve enchanted living, you have to have a good sense of the spiritual experiences that shape your soul, including past lives. Obviously, I'm writing as a believer in reincarnation. Even if you don't believe in life-after-life, however, we can also look to history's lessons as teachers and guides (and there's certainly a lot there to learn and heal from!).

Activity 4.1 - Past Life Viewing

This meditation may take time to master, but it is helpful for tapping into past life memories that can help you in the here and now. If you're someone that does not believe in reincarnation, please adapt the visualization provided so that it focuses on a specific moment or era in history and use that as your starting point for information gathering. I happen to believe we carry a lot of ancestral memory in our genes that will allow us to tap into time's windows no matter from which perspective you approach this activity.

Begin by getting comfortable. Because this meditation may take some time, I recommend lying down. Close your eyes and breathe deeply. See yourself as you are right now in your mind's eye. Envision a golden white light surrounding you, like a womb. Inside that womb, allow the years to turn backward...back five years, 10 years...15 years...until you are an infant again. Then go further. Continue until you are nothing more than spirit outside of body, waiting for a home.

As you become aware of the limitlessness of your form, you also notice a hallway with doors on it. Move your spirit-self down that hallway until you come to a door that somehow calls to you. Pay attention with all your senses to recognize which door most needs to be open at this juncture in your life. From this point in the visualization you can end up at any previous life or any point in history that has some bearing on your current problems, perspectives, needs, and/or goals.

Reach out and open the door. There is a swirling mass of light in front of you, sparkling with all colors of the rainbow. Step through that vortex in time and space. What greets you here is wholly in

Spirit's hands (and those of the mental stage you've set), but pay close attention to the experience. If possible, you may wish to tape record what you see, or write it down afterward so you can meditate on the significance of the images. Bear in mind that it may take days or weeks before an entire portrait and its meaning becomes wholly clear. Also know you can repeat this activity at any time and open new doors!

What Nourishes Wholeness?

Practice 25 (page 17) for enchanted living states that you have to know where you've been to glean a vision for where you're going. Meditations like the previous one help us unlock, view, comprehend, and internalize the past. Using this new understanding as a building block, let's look at the todays.

Awareness is a fresh realization of self as a co-creator with destiny. From this perspective we can ask ourselves, honestly, what is it that nourishes wholeness? What must we release and reclaim? How can we get beyond putting on a plastic veneer of well-being versus integrating a holistic vision to the point where it saturates every cell, every thought, every atom in our aura?

Part of that answer comes in the form of regular care. Spirituality requires "vitamins" too. We need to give our body, mind, and soul nourishing food and proper attention.

Activity 4.2 - The Wholeness Cocoon

Begin this activity much as the last one. Get comfortable, relax, and breathe deeply. Instead of trying to backtrack in time, however, I want you to examine your todays. Where do you work? With whom do you associate as friends or colleagues? What is your home environment like? Look at all the facets of your life, and ask yourself: Is this healthy? Does this nurture wholeness? If not, then it's time to clean out the old and build anew.

One way to accomplish this is to visualize that aspect of your life in literal or symbolic form, then in the visualization turn your back on it. Once you can no longer see that image, begin creating a womb of blue-white energy that rises swirling counter-clockwise from the floor and descends from the sky swirling clockwise. These two spheres meet near your naval, connect, and create a protective cocoon of power in which you can release what you don't need and claim what you do need.

What is the best thing to replace that which you must discard? Bring that into your visualization and don it like a healing salve. For example, if you're in an abusive relationship, the best replacement for that is pure, perfect love. In this case, you could change the color of the light womb to pink for gentle love, or you could see it as the shape of a heart. Alternatively, you might visualize yourself receiving a hug or other types of loving gestures that need no recip-rocation. The key is finding the right image of wholeness to replace that which has harmed.

You can repeat this energy cocoon any time you feel the need, be it the discovery of an unhealthy person, place, or thing in your life. And, even when everything is "good," it's okay to go inside of the transformative energy sphere and reenergize, cleanse away tensions, and emerge refreshed. That too is a spiritual vitamin that nurtures awareness!

This activity brings to bear an important question. What happens when awareness draws our attention to problems, frustrations, sadness, anger, and other negatives? Believe it or not, that's also important. We often sweep such things under the figurative rugs of our soul and let them fester there, causing disease. Instead of allowing this to happen, awareness calls us to act, to recognize the problem, and to fix it. Believe it or not, this can be done without losing our balance!

Activity 4.3 - Remembering Wholeness

Wholeness, in part, begins with an understanding that life will not always be perfect. In such moments, we need to look back to other times, places, and situations that offered happiness, peace, and fulfillment. This is not done to simply wander memory lane or bemoan our present condition by comparison. Instead, this mental jaunt is a way of retrieving some of the good energy from that moment and bring it to the space in which we are currently, to refresh and maintain the pattern of wholeness until the storm blows over. Better still, because the memory can change our overall outlooks and attitudes, the resulting energy shift can repattern the situation to one much more favorable.

To use this activity effectively, you should think about a positive individual or situation that can best give you the kind of energy you need for whatever you're facing presently. For example, if you're trying to overcome anger in a relationship, you'd want to think about a time in that relationship when there was peace and calm resolve. Remember those moments in as much detail as possible, and let the feelings you had then fill you to overflowing. Hold that energy close, like a healing balm, and take it with you into negotiations.

Now, obviously, that's only one example, but it's a good one. Rather than focusing on a negative, you're taking a positive focus into the problem. That, alone, will improve results. Additionally, by reclaiming a "good" pattern instead of clinging to the negative one, you can start fashioning something new using a sound construct. In this example, that may mean changing the dynamics of the relationship, or it could even mean ending the relationship. The Inner Healer recognizes that not all people and situations are healthy for us, but there are ways to end things positively and provide closure. Practice 26 (page 17) for enchanted living states that when we remember and honor wholeness, we can also begin to make our way back to that wholeness.

Awareness keeps one ear to the ground and one toward the Divine, powerfully illustrating the "as above, so below" motto of the Mage. Awareness demands of us acknowledgment, recognition and validation of the wonder in each person, each moment, each miracle. Awareness is open hearted and open minded without falling prey to naiveté and gullibility. Last, but not least, awareness keeps us alert and awake on all levels of being so that we are prepared to act expediently when called into service for the good of all.

SHAMANIC FOCUS: THOUGHTFULNESS

"To live content with small means; to seek elegance
rather than luxury, and refinement rather than
fashion; to be worthy...to study hard, think quietly,
talk gently, act frankly; to listen to the stars and
birds, to babes and sages, with open heart; to bear
all cheerfully, do all bravely, await occasions, hurry
never; in a word to let the spiritual, unbidden and
unconscious, grow up through the common."

—William Henry Channing

Mr. Channing has so eloquently described thoughtful living that I'm almost tempted to leave this section with only those words to ponder. Take a moment to read that quote again, then think of the word thoughtfulness in two parts: "thought" and "fullness." Practice 27 (page 17) for enchanted living is that everything in magick begins in thought and fullness.

Thoughts have power. A metaphysician by the name of Zolar perhaps best stated this when he said, "The power to make and change the mind begins within." How we perceive things, how we think, and how we act on our thoughts makes all the difference in the world. We already talked about perception—being aware—in the keynote section. But what about thinking?

We hear phrases such as "think before you speak" or "think it over" all the time. This indicates that there is a powerful mechanism at work in our minds, and one to which we don't pay enough attention. What's worse is that by not paying attention we often doom ourselves to repeating unproductive, outmoded, unhealthy cycles that do nothing to support our goal of enchanted living.

We often give ourselves over to what I call *trained nega-tivity*: images that fill our thoughts with unrealistic expecta-tions and portraits of what is "good" or "beautiful" or "successful." Thoughtful living discards all that by trusting the inner voice and vision for a self-portrait that's healthy. Frequently, the only thing that stands between you and change is an awareness of your thought processes, recognizing what binds you, releasing those old ways, and then fashioning a whole new spiritual vision in your mind's eye.

Activity 4.4 - Release

For this activity, get a piece of paper and a pen. Give yourself about 20 to 30 minutes of quiet time to think and ponder, specifically about those people, places, and things in your life that don't nurture wholeness. Is there someone who constantly de-means you? Is there some place that always makes you feel uncomfortable? Are there things that sur-round you with bad memories from the past? List them on the paper! Note that you don't have to try to root out every last negative thing in your life all at once, but come up with at least nine items (three people, three places, and three things).

Now, next to each of these, put a goal date, a time frame within which you feel you can make an honest effort mundanely and magickally to change things. For example, if you think it will take a few weeks of talking to the person whose insulting to make them aware of how that hurts you, write two weeks. If a room in your home makes you uncomfortable and you think it will take a month or two to purify the energy (and maybe paint), write two months. Please be realistic here. Setting impossible goals for yourself undermines enchanted living.

Finally put this list in some place of honor in your home (mine went on my altar and my refrigerator door), where you will see it regularly. Each time you see the list, let it nudge you into positive action to begin rooting out the weeds in your life and rebuild gardens of spirit and soul within and without!

Practice Thoughtful Living

While the concept of positive thinking has become almost cliche in the New Age, its ability to build that portrait and to release and sustain the Inner Healer should not be underestimated. For example, the simple affirming phrase, "I can," followed by positive action is an amazing force for change. Practice 28 (page 18) for enchanted living is that each of us participates in our destiny, but only you can determine how much you create, and how much you allow. When you think it, you can *be* it. When you become the thought in fullness, action naturally follows with confidence. This, in turn, establishes all the right components for effective manifestation!

The practice of positive thinking also brings up the concept of mind over matter. In our mental landscape anything is possible. Here you can stretch yourself in new ways, to heights only the imagination can offer. From that thoughtful perspective we begin to reconnect with all time and all possibilities in a whole new way. Practice 29 (page 18) for enchanted living is dare to dream, folks! Dare to believe that your dreams have value, if only by offering a reprieve from the temporal world and glimpse the realm of the creative mind in motion; there, too, is magick!

Thoughtfulness doesn't end with self, however. If anything, that is only the beginning. Thoughtfulness extends to everyone and everything that surrounds us daily. One of the best examples of this comes from the notion of random acts of kindness. Thoughtful living improves our ability to give and receive. It also makes both actions something natural rather than contrived. Better still, every time we thoughtfully give to another, it reaches far beyond that moment and person, sending ripples through all of life's networks, blessing people, places, and things about which you may never know, yet it started with *you*. I can think of no more lovely way to begin releasing and expressing the Healer within.

THE EIGHT-FOLD PATH SPOTLIGHT: RIGHT AND PROPER EFFORT AND LIVELIHOOD

"Genius is only the power of making continuous efforts. The line between failure and success is so fine that we scarcely know when we pass it: so fine that we are often on the line and do not know it. How many a man has thrown up his hands at a time when a little more effort, a little more patience, would have achieved success. As the tide goes out, so it comes clear in. In business, sometimes, prospects may seem darkest when really they are on the turn. A little more persistence, a little more effort, and what seemed hopeless failure may turn to glorious success. There is no failure except in no longer trying. There is no defeat except from within, no really insurmountable barrier save our own inherent weakness of purpose."

—Elbert Hubbard

100

To what do we give our time? What fills our waking and sleeping hours? Things that water wholeness and wholesomeness, and nourish our Inner Healer or things that do not? In looking at the world around, I'd hazard to guess all of us have moments touched by negativity, be it in the form of a person, place, thing, or thought. Right and proper effort strives to make us aware of how wasteful those moments are unless we can transform them somehow. To achieve that positive change, we need to better understand what constitutes "right" effort.

The first lesson embodied by right effort comes in the form of an odd dichotomy. Effort can be both knowing when to act and when to remain still. Part of an old Buddhist story explains this symbolically by saying that one can make beautiful music from a stringed instrument. You can also break the string by having it too tight, or silence the instrument by not tending a loose string. So, we need to know to what to give our efforts, and when, to make the music in our soul sing loud and long.

To provide an illustration, say someone continually comes to a spiritual reader for guidance through a medium like Tarot cards. Every week he or she listens, nods, takes notes, and goes away. Every week the reading is pretty much the same. What constitutes right effort on the part of this psychic (by the way, psychics were some of the original counselors— Healers for the mind and spirit!)? It is certainly not to continue this cycle of unproductive readings. Right effort in this situation would be to instruct the person that before you can help her any more psychically, she needs to *act* on the information she's already received; in other words, you take yourself out of the equation and put the responsibility for personal growth and change back in that person's lap.

This action, in turn, motivates right effort on that person's part too! In effect, it motivates healing if this individual accepts the advice (Practices 19 and 28, pages 16 and 17)!

The second lesson of right effort comes in knowing our limitations. There are things each of us can do, and things we cannot. Practice 30 (page 18) is to accept your weaknesses gracefully, honor your talents with equal poise, then work on both! Right effort always looks to the middle ground between today and tomorrow, between knowledge and intuition, between weakness and strength, between the temporal and eternal.

If we return to the cardinal rule of living in the moment, this balance becomes even more important. Time is fleeting, and it often moves past us before we have the chance to fill out that moment. Yet if we are aware and thoughtful, and putting forth the right effort, that tragedy won't occur. The best way I know of to bring home this lesson is to ponder these wise words by Thich Nhat Hanh from *Present Moment Wonderful Moment*:

> *"Waking up this morning, I smile.*
> *Twenty-four brand new hours are before me.*
> *I vow to live fully in each moment*
> *and to look at all beings with eyes of compassion."*

Activity 4.5 - A Promise

I can't give you the exact way to go about completing this activity because of its personal nature. But right here, and right now, I want you to make a promise to yourself, to others, to the world, and to the Divine to allow awareness, thoughtfulness, and right effort to flow in your life. Whether you make this commitment in prayer, during meditation, or during a private moment of writing, bear in mind the sacredness of this act. It will change you forever.

Remember, a great deal of spirituality begins with allowing, with yielding to the patterns and energy that have been here since the dawn of time (and before). This is not surrender or submission in the societal sense of the term, but instead letting go, and letting God/dess.

Right Livelihood

I should mention at this point that right effort does not discount mundane things in any way. Right effort recognizes that seemingly very tedious tasks (dishes, laundry, etc.) *need* to be done by someone, somewhere. Your right effort may be to become that person! As I said at the beginning of this chapter, the Inner Healer knows the value of little things. If you do your priest's or priestess's dishes, for example, that gives him or her an hour to serve the community. That, my friends, is right effort and a tremendous gift. It also brings us to the idea of right livelihood.

While few of us have spiritually oriented jobs, the Eight-Fold Path and the Healer within emphasize that what we do for a living (our efforts in that job) need to be completed without desecrating our ideals. In fact, our employment should nourish ability, compassion, insight, and joy. Considering the state of our world, exercising the ideal of right and proper employment isn't always easy, but it is very important.

Consider for a moment the kind of energy that your mind produces when it focuses on one thing for 40 hours a week. Now ask yourself what kind of manifestation would come out of that concentration. If your focus includes unhealthy, unhappy, unkind, and unethical circumstances, that is also what will manifest in other areas of your life, based on the law of like attracting like. There is absolutely no way this negativity supports the Healer within!

Let's look at an operative example: A secretary works to support his or her family, and the boss constantly asks the secretary to lie about the budget or other office particulars. Right effort demands honesty, as does truth to self. Right effort also demands responsibility to one's family, and a confrontation could, indeed, cause unemployment. In this situation, the secretary can attempt to minimize deceit as much as possible using diplomacy and start looking for another job that doesn't compromise ethical guidelines. This constitutes right effort and focuses on finding right livelihood, but it may take time to reach a good outcome.

This example brings to bear another aspect of right livelihood. This ideal is not simply a personal matter. The boss's actions affect the secretary. The secretary's manner of handling the boss's demands affect her, everyone she talks to, and everyone with whom she interacts. From there the network continues outward, having rippling effects far beyond what most of us ever imagine. Even if the boss's intentions were good (say to improve the corporate image, improve earnings, and therefore be able to increase salaries), the impression of the lie stays in the subconscious mind and nags at the higher self undermining wholeness. Worse still, the boss has trapped his or her secretary in the same unproductive, unhealthy loop!

Activity 4.6 - Affirming Others

This is an interesting activity that powerfully illustrates the effect of mindful efforts in your workplace. I want you to pick out one person with whom you have trouble interacting (for whatever reason—perhaps they make you uncomfortable, seem like drama queens, or are always grumpy). Now, for one whole week I want you to make gentle, honest efforts to affirm that person in some manner. Compliment her hair, the way he does a particular job; actively search for the good in him or her. This, too, is right effort because it seeks out the best in others, the godself that they can become.

At the end of the week, make an honest appraisal of this person again. Ask yourself: Has your relationship to him or her changed because of your effort? Has that person's outlook changed because of your affirmation? Has the ambiance of your workplace become more positive too? When right effort is applied with love and good intention, it will have these kinds of results.

With this last activity in mind, my best advice on right livelihood is this: Whenever possible, do what you love. When you cannot peruse your bliss, make the most of your employment. Smile; work and walk mindfully through the day. Find ways to encourage others to do likewise, and bring some peace and happiness into their day. When you work in this way, you are acting mindfully, with right effort, and helping everyone around you do likewise.

SENSORY CUES: SMELL AND TOUCH

*"It takes so little to make people happy. Just a touch,
if we know how to give it, just a word fitly spoken,
a slight readjustment of some bolt or pin or bearing
in the delicate machinery of a soul."*

— Frank Crane

105

I must confess that it was extraordinarily difficult to choose among the Healer's most important sensual cues because most truly adept Healers use all of them! I finally settled on these two, feeling that health has an impressive astral aroma (and a physical one) that is easily recognized even by untrained people. This, along with the power of touch to open the Path for wellness, makes a formidable combination.

Smell

In the Far East, it is very common for a Healer to smell a patient in various locations to find telltale signs of disease. Have you ever noticed how a hospital room smells, not just the disinfectant, but the aroma just beyond that. That is the aroma of sickness, and it has a definite energy signature. Mind you, it's interesting to note that it's been a common practice to bring flowers to the ailing for many years, in part because of the more healthful aroma they impart! This concept also ties into aromatherapy as discussed in Chapter 2.

And what about the custom of opening windows to get a breath of fresh air? Doesn't that scent also change the way you feel, your alertness, and the overall ambiance of a whole room? Most people may not think of wind as having an aroma, but it does. Activity 4.6 will help you hone this type of sensual cue.

Activity 4.7 - Smell the Wind

If I can teach you one important lesson in this book, it's Practice 31 (page 18): Take your senses and your spirituality out of the box! It is very easy to get caught up in convention rather than releasing ourselves to something that lies in a dimension just beyond our concrete jungle. That "something" depends on the moment and you, but it's always there.

In this case, I want you to try to extend your sense of smell to people, places, and things where you wouldn't normally consider so doing. Why? To see if they're healthy for you! Use the following four examples as a starting point and make notes of your experiences:

* Go outside on a hot day, a cold day, and a rainy day. Take several deep breaths and identify the differences in aromas each type of day brings; then ask yourself how that changes the overall energy with which you have to work. Also, tie this observation time into other senses. If you could describe the smell as a color, texture, sound, or taste, what would it be?

* Go and pick up a book and fan the pages about three inches from your nose. What does the paper smell like? Now, take this one step further. What do the words and intentions of the author smell like?

* Go to a natural location and find one healthy plant and one that looks sickly (preferably the same type of plant). Smell the sickly one first and make notes of what comes to mind with that scent. Now smell the healthy one. What vibrations make these two plants different? Why is the healthy one vibrant and the other one not? Can you ascertain anything from what your senses are telling you?

* Sit in a location where you can listen to several people. Smell their words. What aromas does each person's speech bear? What does that scent tell you?

In interpreting the impressions you get from aromas, you should always depend on your personal impressions first. If you find yourself wanting in this regard, especially when interacting with others, try using the list that follows here for ideas. Note that the more specific the aroma (like that of pine needles or butter), the more detailed your interpretation can become:

* Sweet: The intensity of the sweetness matters here. A light sweetness is usually positive and uplifting, while a heavy sweetness can indicate falsehood or an overly sentimental nature.
* Sour: Usually not a good sign. Can indicate negativity (for example, a sour disposition) or malady.
* Salty: A wry sense of humor or a situation that can cleans and preserve in some way.
* Spicy: A zest for life, or a situation that offers variety and flavor (but too much could lead to spiritual indigestion!).

The Vital Breath

By the way, it is nearly impossible to separate the sense of smell from the vital breath. Breathing has been used by numerous spiritual traditions as a way of centering, achieving deeper levels of meditative awareness, and for relaxation. If you remember your mom telling you to take a breath and count to 10 when you were angry, you've experienced some of the healing power that comes with metered breathing. In fact, people who have stressful lives would do well to learn a variety of breathing methods. It will decrease anxiety and increase longevity.

Try something right now. Inhale on the count of three, hold your breath for a count of three, then exhale on a count of three. Make sure to fill your lungs from the bottom up (from your diaphragm). As you do this, don't forget to smell the air you're taking into yourself and make a mental note of any lingering vibrations there that you can use, or that you may need to eliminate for health's sake.

Now, how do you feel? Different? Consider exactly what that difference is and quantify it somehow. Remember, awareness is part of the Healer archetype, and the most important person of which you need to remain aware is *you*. We'll be talking more about vital breath with the Air element (Visionary archetype), but for now simply remember that a Healer uses breath as both a tool for personal focus and a means of gathering sensual information. Speaking of which, let's talk about touch.

Touch

The tradition of laying on hands is something we see frequently in metaphysical or religious healing. What is it about hands and touch that brought about such sacred reverence? More than likely, humankind's respect for hands begins very young. As children, it is the hand of a trusted parent that holds, feeds, guides, and comforts us. As we get older, we naturally extend such gestures to others.

As we've already seen, things that have strong social connotations also find their way quickly into the spiritual arena. The conditioned response (both conscious and subconscious) improves the overall effect such gestures will have on us metaphysically. Even beyond this dimension, however, is the very real healing effect touch has physically, emotionally, and mentally. That's why the art of touch therapy has been welcome in the medical community and is presently being taught to nurses, aids, and other health-care professionals globally.

Let's bring the concept of touch home and consider how it can help us tap into and activate our Inner Healer. How often do you touch others on a day-to-day basis, and how often do you avoid it due to social contrivance? Also, ask yourself about how you feel about being touched. Both of these dimensions are important to the holistic portrait. If we never reach past ourselves, we cannot serve the greatest good. And, as we discussed in Practice 24 (page 17), if you don't open yourself to touch, it will be that much harder to touch others effectively. I know some of you are saying, "But I'm just not that touchy-feely." Well, join the club. I've had to practice hugging, touching, and allowing myself to be touched, and it wasn't the least bit easy at first. My best recommendation to others like me is this: Take it slow, and gently increase the kinds of gestures you show to, and accept from, others. Challenge yourself daily to remember things like a hug good-bye before work, or a touch on someone's shoulder when you're talking to show your attention and interest. With time and diligence, it will become much more natural for you.

That having been said, don't overdo it either. There are people in our community who have taboos about whom they can touch intimately (e.g., hug). There are others who are recovering from abusive pasts. Circumstances like this call the Inner Healer to be especially thoughtful and intuitive. When you're not sure, ask! For example, when I'm traveling and meeting a lot of people, I often ask, "Handshake or hug?" Most people just laugh and hug, but not everyone. That simple question alleviates a lot of discomfort (and avoids mishaps neatly).

Additionally, don't allow your enthusiasm for expressing the Inner Healer to vanquish common sense. If you or someone in your immediate family have had colds or the flu, for heavens sake don't give out kisses and hugs! Just politely explain your distance to those who expect more affection. The consideration this shows toward other people's wellness will be much appreciated!

MAGICKAL METHODS: MEDITATION AND PROJECTION

> *"What we plant in the soil of contemplation, we*
> *shall reap in the harvest of action."*
> —Meister Eckhart

Think of meditation and projection like the incoming and outgoing tides. Meditation centers the spirit and soul so it can better channel energy. Projection directs that energy. To understand this more completely in the context of the Healer archetype, let's look at them singularly first.

Meditation

The word *meditation* means "the act of measuring." While the reasons for meditation vary depending on the Path involved, there is always some kind of measure involved: assessing self, evaluating others or circumstances, inspecting psychic abilities, surveying the universe, or pondering the All. The Inner Healers uses this measuring process to look at a person, place, or thing from perspectives not previously considered. While socialized medicine often works in symptomology, meditation seeks out the source. Where one person would lax into mental revelry, the Healer revels in mentality!

Meditation is a practice, meaning that similar to nearly everything else in this book, you won't master it overnight. The reason to practice is quite simple: to measure where our attentiveness and efforts have been misguided and begin redirecting them. Additionally, this time waters the seeds of consciousness and mindfulness to build a foundation of wholeness from which our Inner Healer can grow and blossom.

You cannot change a pattern without understanding it. You cannot understand the pattern by only looking at one dimension of it. Therefore, meditation provides the measure by which you can figuratively see and experience the matrix of things and quantify that matrix. That includes the matrix that is *you*.

Now before this idea sounds too lofty, don't be discouraged. Everyone meditates on some level already. Each time you focus intently on a goal or concentrate on a project, especially when the time seems to fly by unnoticed or people have to poke you several times to get your attention, you've experienced a cursory level of meditation. The only difference between this and what we strive to do in the Healer archetype is intention, the depths achieved, and the ability to maintain this state whether you're sitting, walking, or dancing!

For example, many of us might think of meditation as equating to sitting in such a manner as to look like an elaborate pretzel. Even so, there are a lot of cultures where standing is encouraged. It's considered reverent and alert. This positioning allows one to act if called to service, and it is considered uniquely suited to creative problem solving because it's an active posture.

What about sitting? This posture emphasizes learning and watching. When meditations are aimed at gathering information, especially by observing the Earth's lessons or listening to spirit's voice, this is the perfect position to strike.

And for the Inner Healer? Healing and receiving guidance is best accomplished with a lying meditation. Here your body relaxes completely and allows. We already associate this posture with rest and rejuvenation, so taking it to the spiritual level makes perfect sense. This is also a good posture to assume when seeking visions because we associate lying down with dreaming.

I strongly advocate making meditation a daily practice, even if only for a few minutes. Mind you, don't use meditation as a way to escape the moment; use it to become and embrace the moment, then apply it in the most effective manner possible. In this marvelous mental space, you can become one with all things; you become the pattern of *I Am*. It is from that pattern that projection becomes most effective.

Projection

By definition, *projection* means to extend forward or beyond (in this case with your mind). In alchemy, the powder of projection was a mythic substance sought for transmutation. Combining these two meanings, we get a very powerful image of how projection works and what it does. When a person reaches the pattern of the *I Am* in self and with Spirit, he/she can extend that awareness forward beyond him-/herself, and beyond this moment, to transmute and transform disease into wholeness. This is the essence of magick, and it is an amazing asset for the Healer archetype.

Consider that when we say "extend," that "going beyond" can move forward or backward in time, and through any number of dimensions. Because magick works outside of normal constructs, this projection is certainly viable, but few of us believe in that ability wholly or we would have already transmuted the world. The Inner Healer recognizes that humans often falter in faith, but it is part of his or her job to touch, motivate, and rekindle the soul. That job includes the self (Practice 19 page 17). Without faith, we can do nothing to activate or manifest our Inner Healer, who in turn inspires faith in others. So, in a rather wonderful twist of fate, we're back to Healer, heal thyself.

So how does the mechanism of projection work? That's rather hard to say because each person is a little different. In talking to people, I've found that visualization or physical posturing helps. For example, when person A feels the energy flowing into herself (sustaining personal faith), she might visualize this energy as a blue-white light from above that fills her entire Being from the cellular level up. Once she is filled to overflowing, person A extends her hands palm outward in the direction where she wants to project energy (e.g., toward the person, place, or thing where she wants the energy manifested). From here, the visualization shifts to the same white light pouring in a directional course through the palms on its way. You may find this system works for you too.

It may take some experimentation (Practice 20, page 17) to find what's best for you. Nonetheless, please remember that by moving energy into self first, you not only support belief but also remain responsible for how that energy is eventually used. This brings us to Practice 32 (page 18) for enchanted living: If you don't want responsibility, don't work magick.

ELEMENTAL CORRESPONDENCE: WATER

"When flowing water...meets with obstacles on its path, a blockage in its journey, it pauses. It increases

*in volume and strength, filling up in front of the
obstacle and eventually spilling past it...*

*"Do not turn and run, for there is nowhere
worthwhile for you to go. Do not attempt to push
ahead into the danger...emulate the example of the
water: Pause and build up your strength until the
obstacle no longer represents a blockage."*

—I Ching

Water finds its own shape and way. Try to grasp it in your hands and your success is fleeting. Put it in a container, and it will slowly evaporate, again escaping you. Drink it, freeze it, or boil it, and it transforms. Of all the Elements, Water is the most mutable, teaching us the lesson of flexibility. When we do not flow and bend, we become stagnant or break. The Inner Healer desires that flow because stagnation equates to magickal death, and breaking (quite frankly) hurts! There are plenty of broken people in this world who need to heal, then learn to flow.

Looking back through history, we find individuals around the world honoring or using water in religious ways. People tossed coins in wells to appease Water spirits; some sprinkled out water as a sacred offering or blessing. Others looked to the tides to carry omens and signs, and some stared at the surface of a pool to foretell the future. And considering that the human body's largest base element is water, there's a good reason for this reverence. We simply cannot live without it.

There is also the strong allegorical value of water as a cleansing, refreshing, and nourishing force to consider. That symbolism is why baptism became popular, why some shamans used to float patients in water to overcome disease, and why even today you can find spiritually mindful people taking a bath or shower before entering the sacred space (I'll talk about this more in Sacred Duty in this chapter). Beyond these examples, we also see people using water in spiritual methods and expressions for any one of these types of goals:

* calming a heated temper or relationship.
* improving creative flow.
* aiding personal perception.
* gathering and releasing energy (in meditation projection).
* cleaning the chakra system.
* purifying motivations and ridding negativity.
* nourishing a project or person so the seeds that have been planted, root and grow.

These applications are easier to understand when you realize that the Element of Water is connected with the phases of the moon metaphysically, which were also used in timing ancient healing rites. Water also represents the intuitive nature on which the Inner Healer depends so heavily. But of all of Water's symbols, forms, applications, and powers, there is one that stands out as an expression of the Healer archetype: tears.

Our tears do far more than wash and protect our eyes. They act as a natural release mechanism for emotions. Without that release, people tend to shut down temporarily, then explode like a volcano after time. Keeping our tears inside can also cause more measurable physical harm in the form of stress-related disorders, such as ulcers.

In terms of working with the self, the Healer has to allow tears to flow; otherwise, they'll block a lot of magick.

The flow of tears is like the flow of the ocean. It wears away the rough edges from life, smooths our disposition, relieves anxiety, restores balance, and also acknowledges humanness. Whether tears come as a result of sadness or celebration, in that moment even the most adept of Healers is wholly human, and wholly vulnerable. That scares a lot of us, but it's necessary (per Practices 8 and 24, pages 16 and 17). The Healer who cannot cry is closed down, and therefore unable to help anyone let alone work for the good of all.

I'd like to share a story with you that puts tears in a whole new light. I was about 28 years old, and feeling totally miserable about several things that had gone awry. I quietly slipped out of the house, thinking no one saw me, to cry in private on the porch. Not more than five minutes later, my son found me there, completely in shambles.

At first, I was even more upset because my self-image demanded I show constant strength and assurance to my children (where's that red cape when you need it?). What I didn't realize is that I was building an unrealistic expectation in them, one to which they might eventually hold another person. The expression on his face told me that truth, and it said even more. In that moment, my son saw mommy as a person with needs and faults, as someone who could hurt and understand when he hurt.

That day marked one of the biggest steps I've ever taken toward releasing the Healer within, and it happened by releasing myself from impractical images. As soon as I did, I noticed my son too was crying. So we held each other, and healed each other with our tears. It is a memory I cherish, and I hope the lesson in it helps you too. Practice 33 (page 18) for enchanted living is simply this: Don't put on airs. Dare to let down the walls to laugh, to cry, to *be* human.

SACRED DUTY: CLEANSING

"He who wishes to see how the soul inhabits the body should look to see how that body uses its daily surroundings. If the dwelling is dirty and neglected, the body will be kept by its soul in the same condition, dirty and neglected."

—Leonardo da Vinci

As one reads the sacred books of the world's religions, it seems that going before the Divine in less than pristine condition is akin to placing Minute Rice on your altar. It's considered somewhat rude and gauche. While I suspect that the Sacred Parent is accustomed to dirt (S/he made earth, after all), and probably frets very little over our appearances, this cleanliness changes *our* attitudes and outlooks.

Physical cleanliness exudes a sense of improved well-being. This energy, in turn, improves the vibrations in and around a person's aura, causing what I call the "ah" effect. Have you ever noticed how much better you feel after a long, hot shower or bath, especially when you couldn't get one for a few days? Similarly, how often have you entered a messy or dirty church? The clean body honors self and our physical temple; the clean man-made temple is another sign of respect for the Sacred, but it also signals our subconscious reminding us that something special happens here.

Putting this into the context of the Healer archetype, think for a moment about modern physicians. They wash before working with a patient so there's no exposure to unnecessary germs. In the spiritual setting, this equates to cleaning up our own psychic garbage and knowing how to pick up after folks who litter the astral plane with stray vibrations so some unsuspecting person doesn't get spiritual "germs." Woefully, this is one thing that a lot of us seem to neglect because we've become so accustomed to static and clutter as to be desensitized. If cleanliness is next to godliness, a lot of us have a long way to go to rediscover the God/dess within! This is a trend that needs to stop.

Conclusion

The lessons of this chapter began with awareness and mindfulness, and that includes being alert to times when you or others might not be properly containing or directing energy. Therefore, Practice 34 (page 18) for enchanted living is always clean up your messes; right effort demands nothing less! When you make a mistake, fix it. When you accidentally spread negativity and other psychic clutter in someone else's space, go tidy up! When you harm, heal! Unless you're doing this yourself, don't complain about other's mishaps (Practice 24, page 17). And when you find an unattended mess that's not of your own doing, clean that up too! Goodness knows how long that junk has been laying around like an astral snare for unsuspecting travelers.

In this final action, by dutifully cleansing, you have begun to turn the Sacred Wheel. The Inner Healer is expressing itself in new and wonderful ways, and you are becoming an example that other people can look to, respect, and emulate. You are steering into the Path of the Teacher.

Chapter 5

The Teacher

"A Teacher affects eternity; he can never tell where his influence stops."
—Henry Brooks Adams

Being a Teacher is not an easy calling, yet it is one that we must accept if we're ever going to advance along our spiritual Path. Why? Namely, the first person you teach is *you*. That alone is a very sacred task. Our minds and spirits are nourished by what we give them, by what we accept as truth for our lives. So the first question the Teacher archetype asks is, "What do you consume as soul food?" If you're accepting societal or situational negativity, you might fill up, but it's only junk. There's no real nutrition there; the Inner Healer tells you so (I know, just when you thought you'd get through at least one book without a dietary lecture).

Just as the first task for the Healer archetype was to heal self, the first duty of the Teacher archetype is to fill and expand the mind. You cannot feed people from an empty pot, and you should not feed people things with which you're unacquainted. That's why one of the cardinal rules for spiritual writers is "write what you know and live." Otherwise, we'd be giving people tainted soul food!

Similarly, in the Teacher archetype, one should share from what they know and live. This doesn't mean becoming an expert in all things spiritual. Instead, get to know one or two subjects inside out and backward. We've had the generalities via 101-level books for decades now. It's time for getting down to business and really honing our art! Accomplishing this requires narrowing our focus and researching topics thoroughly.

What topics? That's up to you, but consider your mundane aptitudes and interests, then think about how they might be applied in a spiritual setting. For example, someone with musical ability might teach others how to use a musical instrument as a form of worship or as a means of building energy in the sacred space. Someone with organizational skills might teach others how to best arrange effective spiritually oriented gatherings and festivals.

Activity 5.1 - What to Teach

Right now, ask yourself what talents, pastimes and curiosities fill your life. Try to come up with 10. Write them down on a piece of paper or in a diary. Next to each one write one or two potential spiritual applications. Finally, put these in order from 1-10, number one being the area where you feel most competent, and 10 the least competent. Number one is a good place for your Inner Teacher to begin expressing himself or herself.

I should mention that no matter your skill set, sometimes the universe will ask you to go beyond normal constructs. This happens when a need exists and you're the one who is in the right place at the right time. To site a personal example, a terminally ill friend of mine asked me to help her cross over. Effectively, she wanted me to "teach" her how to let go of life with dignity, how to find a sense of closure and completeness.

I didn't want this job, and certainly felt ill-equipped to handle it, but it was her heart's desire, a desire the universe asked me to honor even though I am not a recognized priestess. So my motto is: Be prepared! By going through this experience, I also learned something incredibly valuable. It is the Teacher within who helps us cope with the unknown, face our fears, and dare to open new horizons, even if the person you're aiding is *you*.

As you can see from Activity 5.1, teaching need not mean writing a book, leading discussion groups, or lecturing (per Practice 31, page 18). Art can teach. Actions can teach. Practice 35 (page 18) for enchanted living, and especially for the Teacher archetype, is to never underestimate the power of a life lived differently. Teaching by example is one of the best methods for quality learning, even in mundania! When that example is uplifting, positive, and motivational, people cannot help but want to emulate it. Yes, there's a heavy responsibility in that, but also tremendous rewards when you see how a small gesture changed someone's life forever, including your own.

KEYNOTE: TIMING

> *"Sometimes being a friend means mastering the art of timing. There is a time for silence, a time to let go and allow people to hurl themselves into their own destiny, and a time to prepare to pick up the pieces when it's all over."*

> — Gloria Naylor

Timing is everything. In spiritual circles, we often say that the Teacher will appear when the student is ready. And in the true spirit of universal humor, this timing is rarely convenient. What is it that makes timing so important to this archetype?

To understand this more fully, we have to flip back the pages of history and look at early mages, seers, and wise people. These people looked to the heavens as influencing life on Earth. Thus they mapped and followed the positions of sun, moon, stars, and other celestial events closely, using these indicators to plant crops, harvest, plan festivals, heal cattle, create travel routes, and improve physical fertility among many other things. Over the eons, this kind of careful watchfulness became an honored tradition. Because it is our desire to plant, harvest, plan, heal, co-create, and improve our spiritual lives, it seems only fitting that some timing be taken into consideration.

To which of these celestial harbingers and other time increments might a spiritual Teacher turn to support his or her efforts? Here are but a few examples:

* Sun: The sun represents the conscious mind to which the Teacher appeals. When it's not possible to be in sunlight, teaching on the sun's day (Sunday) is an alternative as is teaching on Tuesday (Tiw's day), which supports skill and the conscious mind.

* Waxing Moon: This symbolizes growth, especially of the intuitive nature. A good Teacher needs insight, but also wishes to inspire intuitiveness in his or her students.

* Months: March for mastery of materials; May for personal progress; and July to accent the Teacher's leadership skills.

* Moon in Aries: Personal development.
* Moon in Leo: Develop new skills or qualities.
* Moon in Sagittarius: Creating strong foundations, effectively reaching goals.

To put this list into an illustrative example, say a student seems to be having difficulty getting grounded in the work. I'd suggest starting a new lesson when the moon is in Sagittarius to improve the overall foundational energy with which the student is working. Or, if the student has trouble concentrating, I might take him outside in the sunlight to energize his conscious awareness. While these are only examples, they give you a good place to start honoring timing in the way you teach.

The Bible says, in Ecclesiastes 3:1, to everything there is a season and a time to every purpose under heaven. This has some similarities to the magus' worldview, and it neatly ties the Divine into the timing equation. It's interesting to note that many of the world's gods and goddesses who presided over time also ruled human destiny. In this respect, Teachers and the God/dess work together. While a Teacher does not rule destiny, she may certainly have a hand in guiding or influencing it positively.

Speaking of destiny, a good Teacher is also one who has a vision for where other people are headed spiritually. While one always wishes the best for others, our best is not necessarily that person's "best" outcome. As Lao Tzu said in the *Tao Te Ching*, "true mastery can be gained by letting things go their own way. It can't be gained by interfering." This approach and vision allows the Teacher to guide rather than direct, and to impart ideas rather than mandates. It also builds trust between Teacher and student, without which no instruction will really have the greatest effect.

Activity 5.2 - Practicing Gentle Guidance

One of the best ways to learn gentle guidance is in working with children. Children, especially between the ages of 5 to 8, begin to exhibit a kind of determination and stalwart independence. This is also when they start revealing tastes and talents in ways that adults can recognize. So, get to know a child in your life and try to discern what talents that child readily exhibits and find a way to encourage that talent subtly. Make a mental note of how your efforts fare and how it changes that child's activities.

My daughter, for example, loves to draw. But if drawing becomes a chore, she pouts and gets fidgety. If, on the other hand, it becomes a game or I ask her to make something special to put on the refrigerator, her demeanor changes. She gets enthusiastic and very single-minded about that task. In this case, the Teacher in me recognized the power of love, and the natural desire in children for play, as a means of motivating her aptitude.

When Is a Student Ready?

The next obvious question becomes, "What time is the right time?" How does a Teacher recognize the student's readiness, or her own readiness for that matter? More so, for what is he or she ready? The Teacher archetype gains half this insight from the lessons learned on the Healer's side of the Wheel: awareness and mindfulness. If you remain open and aware, you will see people as they truly are. If you are mindful, you will honor that space graciously.

Another portion of the answer to these questions come directly from one's Path. For example, many shamans do not go looking for students; they wait for students to come and ask for learning. In other traditions, students are carefully chosen because of various insights and talents they exhibit. So ask the Teachers of your tradition, those whose words and deeds you respect, what teaching means to them and what, if any, methods exist for finding, choosing, and guiding students.

In addition to the traditional approach, perhaps the best indicator of readiness in any person is simple interest and the willingness to keep an open mind. In Chapter 4, I noted that healing is a cooperative effort. So is teaching. Practice 36 (page 18) for enchanted living is that one must be willing to learn and open to new experiences. Without those two components, it becomes very hard for Spirit to touch you in real and meaningful ways. People who approach spirituality without these characteristics in place basically present a closed door to the universe. And Spirit always honors free will. If your door is closed and locked, it will stay that way until you open it.

Curiosity is also a good indicator that the time is good for teaching. The more curious a person, the more likely she is to dig deep for answers that elude her. The ancient mysteries were called "mysteries" for a good reason! They were enigmatic, elusive, and huge questions that laid heavy on humankind's heart. They still do in many ways. Even in times of such scientific advancement, there is much we do not know. So curiosity encourages the student to look beyond one person or one experience for what truths he accepts. This keeps the student responsible, involved, and away from cultish Teachers.

Be Your Own Guru

The presence of cults and manipulative groups is one very good reason for the Teacher archetype to always acknowledge what he or she does not know. Don't fall prey to the ego trap of trying to have all the answers. I spoke at the outset of this chapter about a Teacher not having to be the wise person who knows the secret of life. Unfortunately, one of the drawbacks about activating the Inner Teacher is that people will begin to put you on a pedestal and think of you as a guru.

There are a lot of people who do not like to think for themselves. It's easier to be led, so there's someone else to blame! Nip this tendency in the bud. Practice 37 (page 18) for enchanted living is that you cannot be anyone else's guru (you already got that job for yourself at Practice 19 (page 17). If a student follows your every word to the letter and begins falling over themselves to emulate your every action, you have a problem! While there might be a normal knee-jerk reaction to a student questioning you on any particular topic, remember that there are no stupid questions except those that remain unasked. Additionally, questions indicate thoughtfulness, interest, and the ability to think for one's self, which are three very good qualities in any pupil.

One of the first things I tell my students is to never believe anything I say as being wholly true. This statement is, at first, met with curious expressions. I then explain that what I'm sharing is what works for me, what has come out of my life and Path. Because I am not them, this experience and the results of same may not be "truth" on another Path or in another setting. This is one of the hard parts of vision-filled traditions. There isn't necessarily a pat right or wrong way to accomplish a goal, nor is there a set time in which that goal *must* be met.

This is the final lesson that timing teaches us: Just as there is a season for all things, there is also a season for all people. One student will not learn or grow at the same pace as another. Spirituality cannot be rushed or forced if it's to have long-lasting results. The Inner Teacher must honor that sense of pace in himself or herself, in others, and in the world.

Shamanic Focus: Reconnect and Integrate

> *"Peace is not won by those who fiercely guard their differences but by those who with open minds and hearts seek out connections."*
> —Katherine Paterson

Teachers find a way to fit things together in their own lives and the lives of others so things work and make sense. Nonetheless, this pattern does little good if it's not implemented in a concrete way. Following with Practice 38 (page 18) for enchanted living, the wise Teacher knows unapplied knowledge is wasteful (if not a tragedy, in my opinion). To keep this from happening, the Teacher archetype depends on reconnection and integration.

Reconnection (to connect again) begins with understanding that all things are bound by invisible threads like a giant tapestry that expands outward through space, time, and dimensions. When you begin to see those strands and how one affects the other, you begin to understand the patterns that weave magick. More so, you also begin to understand your place in that pattern, where your strand has been, and get a vision for where it's going.

In this respect, a Teacher shows us how to reconnect with, or perhaps remember, who and what we are as spiritual beings. The figurative map that a Teacher provides for achieving this goal includes a variety of destinations such as Spirit, the Earth, the ancestors, our tribes, and of course self. The Path to those destinations, however, is chosen by the individual. This brings us back to the awareness that teaching and learning is a cooperative process in which either person may periodically become the Teacher!

Activity 5.3 - Teacher Becomes the Student

I am often amazed by the wisdom and insights many of my new students bring to the table. Their enthusiasm alone is something from which to learn. With this in mind, the next time you're at a gathering of people where you can mingle with some "newbies," do so! Listen to what they're saying. If one stands out as having good concepts, just sit and attend. Don't put your two cents in or try to be the expert in this moment. Allow yourself to be a student again, being filled with all the energy and zeal that a newfound love of spirituality brings. I can almost guarantee you'll come away with fresh perspectives for the effort.

Reconnecting with Self

Returning to the map we've plotted out, let's begin with reconnecting with self. Each student must know himself or herself in the same truthfulness as each archetype emulates. Teachers must regularly remember what it was like to face the self in unvarnished truth (another good reason for the aforementioned activity), and help the student honor that process. This is a good exercise for the Teacher, too, who periodically needs to reconnect with the past to improve the present and work toward the future (per Practice 25, page 17)!

To help with self-reconnection, depend on the Healer archetype to come through in a pinch. The Healer encourages the restoration of the balance and mindfulness necessary to accomplish personal reconnection. The Healer also helps smooth over the inevitable wounds that come from the procedure. Let's face it, few of us really love ourselves completely, let alone *like* ourselves. The process of self-reconnection is designed to create that like and love, that awareness of self-worth (even in the face of obvious faults), and then treasure it as an incredible gift.

Connecting with Tribe

Once the student learns to connect with self honestly, he can begin connecting and reconnecting with others the same way. This is where the tribe and the ancestors come into play. I use *tribe* as a generic term that in the context of this book means a group of people with whom you connect deeply. Using this definition we each have a variety of tribes with whom we interaction. There is the tribe of our blood family, the tribe at work, the tribe of our community, and the tribe of humankind. One of the most important tribes, however, to Healer, Teacher, and student, is that group that we choose to make a part of our life on a long-term basis (be that through friendships, marriage, or other connections).

As we find these people, they become a sustaining, nurturing unit. Healers and Teachers need support because there are a lot of hurting, hungry people in the world. Similarly, the student needs to find a group of which to become part. He or she needs to be integrated into something larger than him- or herself. That something is tribe.

This tribal unit serves several other functions, too. It becomes a Teacher in its own right; group dynamics provide all kinds of opportunities for learning. The strength of the tribe supports and sustains the strength of the entire magickal

131

community. It also helps students keep from wandering too far off track if the other members are living mindfully and have developed the other qualities of the Inner Healer. Such interaction is a fantastic example of how the Sacred Wheel of Healer-Teacher-Warrior-Visionary works together both backward and forward on the Sacred Circle.

Activity 5.4 - Reclaiming a Lost Relationship

Many of us have lost touch with someone that once was important in our life. Be it due to time or distance, or even a tiff, this is a terrible loss. Think about those people and pinpoint one or two that you can still reach by mail, e-mail, phone, or through others. Now, ask yourself what separated you to begin with. How can you "fix" that. If it was an argument, you may need to open the way for apologies or at least calm discussion, but don't hold onto the anger like a badge of honor. If it was distance, then the Internet pretty well solves that equation, as do phones. Reach out and touch someone!

Sometimes we just get so busy with life that we let very special people slip through our hands. Relationships of any nature require ongoing tending to thrive and flourish. Tribes are very real relationships, but I promise you they are more than worth the time and effort.

Connecting with Ancestors

Once a strong connection with tribe is established, honored, and tended, it becomes much easier to open the lines of communication with the ancestors. Ancestral spirits are far more than just memories of those passed over among shamanic cultures. These beings interact with us in specific ways,

132

usually to help with difficult problems or questions. The ancestors are wise people who have walked literally in our shoes, and thus can be great helpmates to the Teacher archetype.

One of the easiest and best ways to start welcoming the ancestors back into your life is by researching your family tree. Find pictures, tokens, and other memorabilia that belonged to your family. Put this reverently on an altar with a glass of fresh water and a white candle (for Spirit). Light the candle on the anniversaries of anyone's death, birth, marriage, and so forth. Also, light it when you're just thinking about those people fondly as a ways of saying hello. Periodically change the water; don't let it become cloudy. This represents the flow of communication and love between the realms.

Once your ancestor altar is functioning, don't be surprised if some of these beings begin to visit you in dreams or meditations. Those two physical and mental states are when it's easiest for spirits to reach us because we are still and listening. Bear in mind that you may not always recognize these beings. Some have a different astral presence, and others are parts of your family you may not know. In either case, however, pay heed to what symbols or words these beings provide. They will feed your Inner Teacher.

The only caution I have is that sometimes spirits have an agenda of their own. Think carefully about those messages and balance them in your mind and heart to be sure they're right for you. Anything that is truth will always return to you again and again, typically through unrelated sources. So if you're not sure, or something seems amiss, trust those instincts.

Making a Place for the Sacred Parent

Going beyond the ancestors in our family line, there are also the ancestors of humankind. These are powerful, universal images of mother, father, sister, and brother that appear in the world's myths. By whatever name you choose to call this Sacred Parent and Source, make a place for him or her in your home and life daily (per Practice 16, page 17). Be it through prayer, meditation, offerings, candle lighting, or other simple gestures, this opens the way for ongoing communication and blessings.

For the Teacher in particular, this interaction is nothing less than necessary because it is his or her duty to guide others into an effective, meaningful rapport with Spirit. You cannot do that if you, yourself, don't understand and honor that rapport (Practice 24, page 17). Additionally, this rapport provides the perfect medium through which Spirit can speak to a student's heart in ways the Teacher might not normally consider or attempt.

For example, it is quite common for good Teachers to completely ignore lesson notes when speaking publicly because Spirit begins to take the lecture in a different direction. This shift is something one senses; it's hard to describe, but it is very definitive, similar to making a sudden turn on a road. At this juncture, the Teacher relinquishes the proverbial driver's seat to the Sacred, and sits back to listen!

I've also experienced something like this when writing, when I complete whole paragraphs of which I have no memory. Reading them, I find I'm learning whole new concepts, or minimally a new approach to an established ideal. This is Spirit's maker's mark, a fingerprint of sorts, and the Teacher archetype recognizes it because he or she is already reconnected and maintaining a strong relationship with the Maker.

Transforming Ourselves through Reconnection

Now let's look at integration. To me, integration is a fancy word for making something real. All our reconnection, all our wisdom, all our learning, means very little if we don't let all these things seep into our very souls and transform us from inside out. That transformation is also an activating process; it takes spiritual lessons and manifests them into living, breathing, motion in our daily lives.

A Teacher's job is to encourage that internalization by periodically pausing the learning process so that everything has the chance to settle into place. We can cram our heads full of information, but when it never reaches heart and soul, it is only "mental" knowledge, not true spiritual learning. Additionally, one can reach a spot in the learning process where this ongoing mental buildup creates a kind of critical mass, meaning use it, appreciate it, or lose it, which also happens to be Practice 39 (page 18) of enchanted living!

In this respect timing and internalization work together. Each of us should begin to recognize those moments when we need to take what life and our studies have imprinted in the mind, and make them *real*. At that critical juncture stop, breathe, meditate, *become* what you have learned in word and deed. Be you a Teacher or a student, don't continue until you see that knowledge manifest in concrete ways in your life.

THE EIGHT-FOLD PATH SPOTLIGHT: VIEW AND THINKING

> *"I don't pretend we have all the answers. But the questions are certainly worth thinking about."*
> —Arthur C. Clarke

One of the great gifts of the Teacher archetype is perspective: being able to show people new ways to see and think about a variety of things. There is very little wholly original under the sun, yet by looking at the old in new ways, we can create originality and freshness. And for those wonders that technology is bringing us, the Inner Teacher sees potential there and shares that discernment with others. But be it an item or idea, old or new, it is always a matter of view and thinking that makes it magickal!

Activity 5.5 - A New Way of Seeing

Find a multifaceted crystal and put it on a plain cloth in front of you. Observe it from where you are right now, extending all your senses into this observation. Once you've gathered as much insight as you can, move yourself to another location, perhaps 30 degrees from where you are now, and look at the crystal again. How has that movement changed your view, both physically and metaphysically? The awareness that everything in life has more than one figurative "side" to it is part of what right view teaches us. Until we see all the sides, our perspective will be flawed.

Right View

Right view begins with understanding, having the faith and confidence to look at things differently and truly see them. Each of us has the ability to transform our reality if we can recognize the seeds of negativity and weed them out, and cultivate the positive ones. The Teacher's calling is to help a student identify those seeds, and then provide the right tools for him or her to begin making changes.

Right view goes further beyond simple understanding, however. This process wakes us up to potentialities. Here the mindfulness of the Healer reaches into the Teacher archetype and says, "Watch and learn." Our perceptions of reality and of what truly exists on all dimensions are often two different things. Take the example of Superman. The only thing that separated this powerful being from Clark Kent to mortal eyes were a pair of glasses. Was this truly a competent disguise? Of course not! People chose to see the part of truth with which they could cope.

In spiritual circles, right viewing is painfully evident among those religions that want to dictate rather than guide. The people in these groups embrace and water fear rather than celebrating the many paths to the One. This happens quite naturally because, for one, it is simply easier to believe we are right; there is comfort in that egotism. For another thing, we usually perceive things very subjectively as outside the self. In Buddhism, however, right view means that when you look at the stars, they are you. When you look at another person or Path, they are you. In this manner, the Teacher can walk a mile in the student's shoes so as to teach more effectively.

Releasing Conceptual Perceptions

The whole reason we use the phrase "point of view" is because of individual subjectivity. However, to be a really *good* Teacher (and an adept spiritual being), we often have to release our conceptual perceptions and simply allow. From this stance, one is part of the All, all is part of the One, both are wholly correct, and both are in *motion*. Effectively, right mindfulness, combined with right view, puts knowledge into action.

Right view follows this basic process: learn, reflect, practice. Learning the right way of perceiving self, the world, and Spirit gives you much food for thought. This spiritual nourishment marks the perfect stopping point for integration and reflection on the lesson(s). Then, quite naturally, putting the lesson into practice makes perfect sense so that the internal is externalized in a living, breathing, meaningful way.

Right Thinking

It is because of right view's process that we must consider right thinking. How can you reflect and internalize without right thinking? Thought is nothing more than the speech of your mind. The more precise and positive those words become, the more precise and positive the results (the practical applications) become.

Mind you, right thinking isn't easy. Our minds are often busy doing one thing while our bodies are doing another, and unless we take mental speech and unite it with action, we can't get to applying what we've learned! The main way that Eastern systems help students get body and mind into harmony is through rhythmic, even breathing. Breath is life. Breath honors the moment you're in. Breath is being. Stop right now and just breath deeply and evenly for a few minutes. Enjoy the freshness in that breath. Feel it activating your Inner Healer for mindfulness. Now, reread the last paragraph. Get something different out of it? Willing to bet you did!

Thought is complicated, however, by the fact that there are two distinct types of thinking. First is the initial thought, and second is developmental thought. The initial thought tends toward the concrete, logical formulation. For example, one might think, "Today I have to go to work." The developmental thought, however, goes further. It asks, "Is the way I'm driving to work the most expedient path? Should I go more quickly? Could I bus to save on gas?" When we breathe and meditate, it releases the Inner Teacher to help us form both the initial and developmental thoughts more effectively. And, at some point in the meditative process, *both* these stages are released into being and action (exactly at what point depends much on the individual).

Practices of Right Thinking

Right thinking breaks down to four distinct practices. The first is for both the Teacher and student to ask, "Am I certain?" If the Teacher isn't sure, then he or she shouldn't say word one! If the student isn't sure, then he or she is most likely with the wrong Teacher or walking the wrong Path. Before you go anywhere or integrate "truth" as yourself, ask, "Are you sure?"

The second practice is asking, "What am I doing?" And I might even presume to add to this question: Why are you doing it? There is no reason to rush in spiritual pursuits. Quality learning often takes time, so if you find yourself rushing when you ask this question, stop and slow down! The Healer's mindfulness here keeps you in the moment, and allows all things to take their own time (ah, there's that Teacher's catch word, *time*, again). Add the whys into the equation, and you remember from where you've come and the fire that ignited your soul. What this practice accomplishes is nothing less than making every moment sacred, every act sacred; it turns your entire existence into a living, breathing, moving temple (Practice 17, page 17)!

The third practice is asking, "Am I doing this out of habit?" All of us have little rituals we follow to make life's ebb and flow familiar and welcoming. Nonetheless, not all these rituals are good for us. For example, my Type A personality habit/ritual of working nonstop accomplishes a great deal, but it isn't always good for me. Sometimes, I need to stop and breathe, stop and appreciate a sunset or the wonder of simply being still for a moment. But that stopping won't happen naturally until I accept my habits and no longer allow them to rule me and my thoughts.

Finally, the last practice is that of treasuring the mind of love. The Healer facilitates mindfulness, the Teacher facilitates that same mindfulness with love as a foundation, which becomes a potent force for change. You cannot liberate the mind that does not know how to give and receive love or see things with the mind of love, for that person is still bound to old ways of interpreting reality. Once you let love out of the box, however, everything changes. Practice 40 (page 18) for enchanted living, therefore, is simply to cultivate the mind of perfect love. When you replace anger, insecurity, fear, bitterness, and other negatives with love, miracles become not only possible, but probable!

SENSORY CUES: TASTE AND VOICE

"You've got to work on your voice, it's your tool and represents you. It's very important to have a good voice where you can be understood."

— Jacqueline Bisset

Every word we speak has a distinctive flavor and texture to it. Some are bitter, some sweet, some smooth, some crunchy. That very same flavor and texture influences the ways in which our words are interpreted by others. Thus we come to the crux of why the sense of taste is important to the Teacher archetype.

While books can teach much, there is nothing quite so amazing as a Teacher who knows how to speak using richly flavored words and a powerful voice. I wrote earlier in this chapter about how a good Teacher will often relinquish his or her planned words so that Spirit can flow. Even when those magickal moments don't come, a Teacher knows how to communicate ideas verbally, not just for the sake of hearing, but for understanding!

Now I am aware that many of us are not wholly comfortable with the sound of our own voice. This is an obstacle for the Teacher archetype, and one that can be overcome with practice. Find a book that you enjoy and read it aloud while taping yourself. Now listen to that tape. If you could change your delivery in any way to make the listening process more engaging and savory, what would you do? Try again and make those changes. Practice like this will make you a better communicator not just when you're teaching, but in all your personal interactions.

Listening Skills

Another way to help improve your communication skills is to borrow a talent from the next archetype on the Wheel, the Warrior's hearing. As you will learn in Chapter 6, the Warrior depends on keen listening skills to know when to act and when to remain still. The Teacher can utilize this listening ability to know what to say and how to say it so the information is received in the best possible manner.

It's hard to describe this skill. For lack of better words, it's like watching yourself from the outside, using your astral senses to see and hear yourself as you deliver a lesson. And don't leave your astral taste buds out of this process. Feel the flavor and energy your words are delivering. If you don't like the way they taste, your audience likely won't either! Now, that doesn't mean that everything you teach has to be sweet

141

and gentle. Spiritual lessons have some harsh realities attached. The key here is finding a way to impart knowledge so it builds rather than destroys; in other words, balance the sour with the sweet in the right proportions so the hard parts are easier to swallow and integrate.

The Power of Humor

One of the best tools for serving up difficult lessons is a healthy dose of humor. I am a firm believer in the power of humor to teach, heal, motivate, and initiate. Practice 41 (page 18) of enchanted living is that humor is good soul food! An adept Teacher can use this figurative food to fill spiritual hunger while neatly taming the taste of austere, arduous, or painful lessons that act as our spiritual refining fires.

Anyone who tells you that living an adept magickal lifestyle makes things easier obviously has *not* lived this Path. There are trials and snares on any Path worth walking. These obstacles exist as growth-oriented experiences, as things that hone the soul. Without the challenges we wouldn't appreciate our magick anywhere near as much; that is simply human nature. But with the Teacher's humor to sustain and uplift us, even large potholes in our path can be overcome. This isn't always easy, but humor helps us remember that on the other side of that darkness the Inner Healer is still there, remembering the pattern of wholeness.

MAGICKAL METHODS: DISCIPLINE, STORYTELLING, REPATTERNING

> *"Storytelling reveals meaning without committing the error of defining it."*
>
> —Hannah Arendt

Teachers must not only fit things together properly, they have to provide a means to express and act upon the new portrait of reality created by that process (per Practice 38, page 18). Discipline, storytelling, and repatterning are three methods that accomplish just that.

The purpose behind all three is to transform those things in our spiritual realities that are overcultivated or underdeveloped, and begin reestablishing balance (something the Healer can help us with too). Say, for example, a student always bemoans a specific fault. The Teacher provides constructive criticism for that fault, and adds to the critique a point of esteem. This point balances the negative and provides a positive focus, but that alone is not enough. Now the Teacher has to provide an application, something that inspires the student to relinquish the old and welcome the new vision. That exercise or activity will likely integrate discipline (focus and staying on task), storytelling (examples), and repatterning (transforming old ways).

Discipline

Before we can combine the three, however, we need to have a firm grasp of each individually. Of the three, I personally feel that discipline is among the hardest to master for most people. I see an awful lot of folks in the magickal community who want what they perceive as the perks of spirituality without any of the work. Practice 42 (page 18) for enchanted living states that hard work is *very* good magick. Discipline drives and guides hard work, and it also makes the results from that work more fruitful!

I find it interesting that the word *discipline* comes from a Latin term that means "to learn or train," two things that apply to the student and Teacher directly! Secondary meanings

143

are just as insightful: to submit, correct, inform, prepare, and regulate. The Teacher submits himself or herself to the service of the greatest good and Spirit. The student, in a limited sense, submits himself or herself to the Teacher for instruction.

The Teacher uses knowledge to correct misconceptions and misinformation. She also prepares the student for the Path ahead, while the student regulates his progress according to the call of his soul. Unfortunately, while a Teacher should be disciplined in her methods, the core of discipline is not something that can actually be taught to anyone. It's something we must determine to cultivate, and then stick to it!

Perhaps the most important lesson that discipline teaches, however, is that practice makes perfect. Even Buddha recognized this when he said (paraphrased) that most things in life boil down to three words: practice, practice, practice. Discipline furnishes the diligence with which to get up and start again when we fall. Discipline says, "I will not give up on myself or my magick." Once we reach this resolute point, we can then turn to storytelling as a helpmate in reaching our educational goals.

Storytelling

Stepping back into a shamanic viewpoint for a minute, a story is a means of communicating ethics, values, beliefs, and traditions through illustration. The Teacher archetype uses stories (preferably those from personal experience) to bring an idea home to the heart. There are a lot of concepts in our spiritual journey that seem blurry when we first hear about them. The nonlinear, visionary nature of our spiritual quest challenges the rational mind. A story, however, appeals to the rational self and gives our mind something to wrap around and hold tight.

To give you a functional example, when I teach about spells, I'm very contentious about explaining the need for sensual cues, details, and specifics in our constructs. Now, we also often tell students that intention is the most important part of spells, so it's understandable that some pupils would be confused when you begin to discuss minute particulars as having such significance. When someone experiences that confusion, I rely on an experience (the story) relayed to me from a lovely young lady at a conference. She told me of the spell she cast for a perfect companion. She timed it right, laid out the hair color, eye color and personality she desired, but forgot one small detail: species. She now has the best dog anyone could want (yes, the hair color, eye color, and personality all matched the spell). Now, do you see how a story like that helps clarify a point? It also shows us quite plainly that the universe has a wicked sense of humor!

Activity 5.6 - A Story Diary

Find a medium in which you like to record spiritual information (computer, tape recording, paper, or whatever). As you hear stories or live through experiences that have a specific lesson, illustration, or example to offer, begin transcribing them. I suggest so doing with some kind of title or theme to which you can refer in the future when you need a good story to help make a point. Over time you'll likely want to memorize these too (stories are much better when told from memory so you're focused on illustrating your theme instead of a piece of paper with notes!). Also bear in mind that as you share these stories with your students, you're creating a kind of tradition. They, in turn, will often fall back on your narratives when their wheel comes round to the Teacher archetype.

Another function of storytelling in teaching is motivating right action (another Warrior attribute), and getting people to apply knowledge. After all, most people find it much easier to act when they hear an inspiring tale that shows how a similar action manifested in success. What's really neat here is that this applied knowledge, expressed via action, takes right thinking and view and gives them an outlet that's personalized and fulfilling. What a great gift to give ourselves or another!

While stories need not always be based in truth, they should bear strong elements of truth so that people can sense it. They should also have good imagery so the listener can visualize details. The reason for both becomes more apparent when we begin talking about using storytelling as a tool for repatterning.

Repatterning

Repatterning has two different aspects. The first is changing the rituals and habits we presently enact, specifically those that are unproductive or harmful. Humans are creatures who love making patterns. We pattern our mornings by getting out of the same side of the bed, using the same coffee cup, and driving to work by the same route. When those patterns don't happen just right, our entire day feels out of sorts. Nonetheless, there are some patterns in our lives that can, and should, change.

Ritualistic or habitual repatterning begins by determining the specific negative along with all the surrounding details that generate that negative. For example, if you constantly bite your fingernails, you need to not only be aware of that action as it occurs to stop it, but also what causes that action. By activating the Inner Healer's mindfulness, and avoiding

146

the cause (repatterning), you can start successfully banishing the habit. Effectively, you learn a whole new way of working through the situations that cause the negative ritual/habit!

The second aspect of repatterning is that of mentally changing the outcome of a situation. Because shamans trust that life is what we *think* it to be, repatterning goes to the root of the matter and works hand-in-hand with right thinking! Take the example of someone having a nasty break-up in a relationship that has left them drained and vulnerable. A Teacher can help that person repattern that experience by a guided meditation that reviews the break-up, but replaces the negative words and actions with a less harsh scenario through storytelling and visualization.

While this kind of memory repatterning will not change the ultimate outcome of that situation (the end of the relationship), it will open an alternative Path to wholeness for that person. Repatterning provides a new mental construct on which to focus. When we're receptive (remember healing requires participation) our entire being can respond to that new image (per Practice 26, page 17). At this juncture, the Inner Healer takes over to finish the process.

Right Thinking and Repatterning

By the way, before you begin to work with repatterning for yourself or others, return to Chapter 1 for a moment and review the section on the Patterns of Power. This section helps in recognizing the pattern with which you have to work so that you can find the best way to transform it. Also, bear in mind that using habitual and mental transformation in tandem improves results. A person who visualizes a positive outcome, then takes action to support that outcome, is far more likely to experience success.

The only caution here is to rely on the Inner Healer's common sense in repatterning. The phrase "putting a square peg in a round hole" comes to mind by way of explaining the importance of right thinking at this juncture. Teachers rely heavily on the conscious mind and rationality for the conveyance and internalization of lessons. While miracles do happen, some patterns simply are not meant to be, and others are not good for us. Wisdom comes from identifying which is which.

Let's return to the previous example of a broken relationship. If a couple's pattern together is unhealthy and harmful, then the *right* pattern for that situation is singularity, both people moving into separate paths and a new pattern alone. The repatterning exercise for this situation should, therefore, focus on healing the individual's heart and the beginning of a new life, rather than trying to hang onto the old construct. In this scenario, Inner Teacher's ability to think and view things differently helps us get past our sadness, and sort good patterns from bad patterns. From here action follows thought, taking one step at a time toward wholeness.

ELEMENTAL CORRESPONDENCE: EARTH

> *"Earth's crammed with heaven, And every common bush afire with God; But only he who sees, takes off his shoes—The rest sit round it and pluck blackberries. . . ."*
>
> —Elizabeth Barrett Browning

Many of the world's myths talk of humans being made from dirt, mud, or clay. Spiritually, the Earth is our mother and our classroom for learning. Metaphysically, Earth represents foundation, grounding, growth, maturity, skill cultivation, and sustenance. Additionally, the Earth element touches all other Elements: the winds are the Earth's breath, the rain, its tears, and the sun, its fire. One handful of soil holds all of creation's greatest powers and insights. With this in mind, it's not surprising to find the Teacher archetype intimately intertwined with this Element.

Activity 5.7 - The Tree of Self

This is a visualization/meditation. For those of you who have trouble grabbing on to images without vocal guidance, you might want to tape record this activity and play it back when you're in a suitably focused frame of mind.

Begin by standing. I suggest putting your back against a wall as it will support you throughout the meditation (some people find they get a little dizzy). Next, take several deep breaths in through your nose and out through your mouth. Close your eyes and let the world around you fade away. There is nothing now, no worries or tensions, only the sound of your breathing and the beating of your heart.

Visualize yourself as you stand now. Beginning at your head, slowly imagine your hair turning into leaves and your skin becoming the texture of bark. Trust in the wall behind you to become part of your trunk. As you feel that strength and security building, look down toward your feet and observe them turning into a large network of roots that grasp the Earth with a loving embrace. The soil is cool and welcoming, and filled with nourishment. This spirit, this body, this tree of self is now wholly connected to the Earth element.

Feel it sustain you. Feel the waters seeping out and into your roots. Feel how it gives you foundations. Taste its richness; smell its fertility. The Teacher's tree of self can put down these roots any time there's a need and feast on Earth's abundant patience, wisdom, and stability.

Foundation and Balance

Beyond turning to the Earth element as a source, the Teacher archetype utilizes Earth as a helpmate and a classroom. Where the Healer worked with Water to remove blockages, cleanse, and nourish, the Teacher works with Earth to keep our feet on solid ground and as an abundant font of lesson material. Metaphysical studies can lead someone to an excess of wool gathering and flights of fancy. Our spirit naturally seeks freedom and wants to spread its wings. Nonetheless, without a foundation in which to grow, without balancing the mundane and the mystical, we can't really experience that liberation. Earth furnishes both the foundations and the balance that all of us need, including the Teacher!

Exactly how each Teacher utilizes the Earth varies. My favorite method is simply to get people sitting together on the floor or a flat grassy area. From this position everyone is more grounded and on equal footing. I've also found this seems to relax people, who then open up, and just share. The more open and flowing the dialogue is, the higher quality the learning becomes, and that's not just for the student. A mindful Teacher can learn much from this exchange too (fulfilling Practices 28, 33, and 36, page 18)!

SACRED DUTY: PILGRIMAGE

*"As I make my slow pilgrimage through the
world, a certain sense of beautiful mystery seems
to gather and grow."*
—A. C. Benson, *From a College Window*

For a Teacher to have global vision, it helps to travel beyond your own backyard. A pilgrimage, however, is more than a merry jaunt in the countryside or a European vacation. It is the journey of the soul toward discovery, and an expression of respect to Spirit, be it the Great Spirit or the spirit of place.

A pilgrimage is an initiation of sorts. It marks the beginning of a special journey that isn't just physical; it's spiritual, and it supports the Inner Teacher. But because most of us aren't about to go to Mecca, the question remains of what constitutes a Teacher's pilgrimage and what processes take place during it. This isn't an easy question to answer because it can be as unique as each individual. Thus, I'm going to try to define the act and its processes in somewhat generic terms.

A pilgrimage is a quest in which the journey is just as important as the destination. While most pilgrimages move toward a sacred place for devotional purposes, what defines this sacredness and purpose can only be determined in the altar of one's heart. Some faiths even go so far as to define all of life as a pilgrimage, and I happen to agree.

Even on a slightly smaller scale than that of life's sojourn, a pilgrimage presents challenges and ideas, and it stretches human consciousness and tenacity in new ways. That is part of the journey's goal. We don't want to simply reach a physical place, but arrive at a spiritual nexus, too. The obstacles and physical, mental, and spiritual maneuvering of a pilgrimage help shape that nexus.

Understanding the Pilgrimage

As the saying goes, even the longest journeys begin with one step. That first step is personal readiness, which brings us back to the Teacher's gift of timing. A pilgrimage should take place when you are rested, focused, and when you truly have the time to integrate and appreciate the experience. Additionally, a pilgrimage might be best scheduled at a personally significant time, like before an important initiation, or on your birthday.

The second step of the pilgrimage is knowing to where you wish to go. In making the choice of where, remember that distance isn't a factor. A trip around the corner to a childhood friend's house can be incredibly meaningful, as can a walk to a nearby park where you feel connected to Earth, or an excursion around the globe! Most importantly, the destination should somehow mirror your goals for the trek, as does the path by which you go. For example, say you decided to go on a pilgrimage to a wooded area to become more attuned to nature and her lessons. You'd want to choose a somewhat remote area where the concrete jungle wouldn't hinder perception. Also, you might actually want to hike to this region instead of taking a car, because the automobile isn't as Earth friendly. In this case, the means of transportation doesn't support your goal and requires some creative thought.

The third step, which works in tandem with the second, is *why* you're undertaking a pilgrimage and *what you hope to achieve* through the journey. Keep the whys and your purpose in the forefront of your mind throughout the adventure, no matter how short or long it may be. From this point forward, it is a matter of quieting your mind, breathing deeply, and moving slowly. This is not the time to rush blindly. In fact, leave your watch behind, if practicable. Disconnect from mundane constructs long enough to really reconnect (in a true Teacher's fashion) with yourself and Spirit.

Speaking of which, Spirit is a partner with you on this journey. Remain open to what that power wishes to reveal. Remember that while you may have a set purpose in mind, let go and let God/dess! That kind of release allows the pilgrimage to blossom into a life-changing experience, one that you'll likely rely on in storytelling again and again.

CONCLUSION

The Teacher's pilgrimage often results in the wheel turning once again. After seeing the wonders of Earth and all its spiritual wisdom, it's nearly impossible not to feel some sense of protectiveness swell within. Knowing what we stand to lose by ignoring our magick, and the magick in all things, is the spark that fuels the Warrior, who we will now explore.

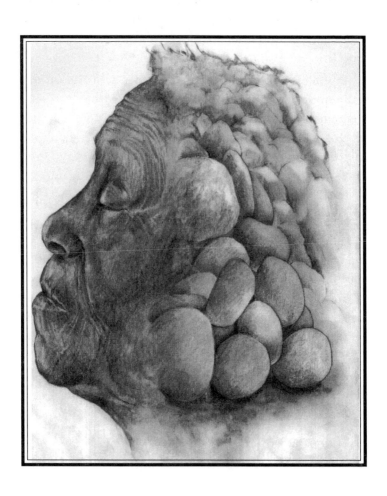

Chapter 6

The Warrior

"The two most powerful warriors are patience and time."

—Leo Tolstoy

It's no coincidence that the Warrior archetype starts out with the patience of the Healer and the time of the Teacher. He or she has steered through those Paths, and the associated lessons have become a coping mechanism and helpmate for this archetype's responsibilities. The duties of the Warrior are demanding, and their burdens are often heavy. They uphold nothing less than the safety and reputation of the spiritual community (or at least their corner of it).

Exactly what form this defense takes depends greatly on you. Practice 42 (page 18) for enchanted living is that the universe always uses the best skill sets we have for the task at hand to effect change. For example, if you have strong writing skills, you might defend religious liberty through letter or speech writing. While we might not immediately consider this kind of action as being typical of a Warrior, think about the old saying that "the pen is mightier than the sword!" Old sayings become old sayings for very good reasons.

Building on this idea and Practice 31 (page 18}, don't constrain yourself to any preconceived notions of what constitutes a Warrior. I know I was very surprised when I first started studying this archetype. My ingrained image of the Warrior was that of someone (male) who is forever riding off on quests, with sword drawn. Because I am female, dislike confrontation and battle (and avoid both like the plague), this was a very difficult image for me to relate to on a personal level, let alone emulate.

What helped me overcome my misgivings and preconceived notions about this archetype? The wonderful school of life experience. As I became more intimately involved with my spiritual community, I also became aware of moments when the liberties or security of some in that community (or in my personal tribe) were threatened. These moments instinctively ignited my inner Warrior, or at least her desire to *act*.

The first few times this happened, I wasn't really sure what to do with the associated energy and feelings, which burned like a pot-bellied stove in my soul. All I knew is that I had this power and wanted to do something, but I needed to make sure it was the *right* something. Thankfully, I was wise enough (or scared enough) to believe that a spiritual Warrior cannot rush blindly in, nor should she allow personal desires and feelings to intrude on a task.

I learned a lot from those first few experiences. The most important lesson of all was that being a spiritual soldier has a lot more to do with wisdom than war, and that awareness made all the difference in the world. Yes, historically a good Warrior needed a fast mind, able body, and personal aptitude, but in the modern spiritual setting willingness, openness, awareness, and common sense seem just as important.

Activity 6.1 - How Do You See the Warrior?

For this activity, I'd like you to try some free-flow writing. Ask yourself how you would describe a spiritual Warrior. What do you think are the associated rights and responsibilities of this archetype? Do you see any characteristics of your perception of a Warrior already within yourself. If so, what are they? Keep this writing somewhere safe until you complete this chapter.

After reading the entire chapter, review the original material you wrote and make notes about how your perceptions have changed. Consider what in your life's experiences created your original views, and what chords this chapter struck in your own spirit. This will help you better understand, identify, and activate your own Inner Warrior.

Ultimately, a Warrior defends truth, honor, and freedom. To accomplish this, the first duty of the Warrior is to cultivate a healthy respect for others along with a good dose of erudition. In fact, I'd say this is a good task for all spiritual seekers. Why? Because the power associated with both magick and the Warrior archetype can benefit or harm depending on how it's wielded. So before rushing in hastily, we should exercise self-control by stopping for a moment, measuring, and evaluating the best path for victory in any given situation through the heart of the Healer and the eyes of the Teacher. In this manner, the Warrior's heart and soul is still one of peacekeeping and security, while his or her hands are those of action.

KEYNOTE: READINESS AND MOVEMENT

*"We have too many high-sounding words, and too
few actions that correspond with them."*

— Abigail Adams

Being ready to act and actually moving into action are
two very different matters. The Warrior knows full well that
there are some limits and boundaries over which he or she
should not cross (per Practice 30, page 18). Each person has
defined margins in life, and for the Warrior these come in
the form of taboos, and in knowing for what causes he/she
will fight.

Margins also come in the form of realizing that some
things will never be as we wish them. Like every other archetype, the Warrior has conditioned perceptions and thoughts
about a variety of subjects, not all of which are true. Nonetheless, the Warrior must be ready, willing, and able to set aside
those preconceived notions and work for the good of all.

Readiness is a state in which all of these margins hover
heavily in the Warriors mind and spirit. Just because one is
ready to fight, doesn't make the fight "right." Readiness has
several other aspects, too, the first of which is courage. To be
ready to act when called upon to do so requires tremendous
courage and a strong sense of self. Otherwise, there would be
a tendency to hesitate and falter during critical moments;
necessary movement would be interrupted.

Second, readiness asks that while the Warrior should not
waver in his or her duties, he or she should move at the right
speed for the situation at hand. The saying, "Fools rush in
where angels fear to tread," is a good one for the Warrior to
remember. Not all fights are won quickly, and some require

slow tenacity just to make progress! Here we see another example of the Teacher's sense of timing coming in very handy in the next archetype on the wheel. Timing is, indeed, everything and perhaps even more so for the Warrior than the Teacher!

Third, readiness returns to Practice 6 (page 16): Know thyself. The Warrior must know to where his or her skills are best suited. A good Warrior doesn't expend energy needlessly. Knowing when, where, and why he/she should be doing a job conserves power. Conservation comes in a variety of forms:

* Knowing which battles are worth fighting.
* Knowing for which battles you're not suited (this includes bowing out of ones in which your emotions will become clouded).
* Knowing which battles you cannot fight due to personal boundaries and taboos.
* Knowing when and where to enter the battle.
* Knowing when to make a gracious retreat for your sake, or the sake of those beside you.
* Knowing when to put down the sword altogether and make peace.

Accomplishing this kind of power conservation isn't necessarily easy. Just as sure as a Warrior needs ready confidence to go into battle, the kind of confidence required to stay out of a situation or make peace is equally so. Why? Well, just ask yourself what happens if and when the Warrior is wrong. In this respect, readiness boils down to one word: trust. It's not hoping that you'll win, or hoping you're right; it's trusting that whatever you do constitutes right action.

Too many of us give away our personal power (and thus our readiness) when we use phrases such as "I can't," or "There's

159

no use," or "I wish." The first two verbal patterns dwell on a negative or depreciating quality. The third isn't active, and readiness means being prepared to *act*. Our thoughts and words must also be ready.

Activity 6.2 - Speaking with Power

Every person's time constraints differ. For this activity, consider a time period during which you can be very focused on your thoughts and speech. I'd recommend at least one day, and preferably a week, but choose a span to which you can commit.

Next, during that time frame pay very close attention to the way you think and speak, watching for patterns that rob you of your power. For example, I tend to be an apologizer; I apologize for everything (even stuff that's not my fault). This is a coping mechanism for poor self-esteem, and it robs me of my power over situations where I could have an effect. Other people are dreamers who never act, others still are actors who never get real nor do they ever dare to dream! There is a balance in all things, and this is your chance to find it in your thoughts, and how you express yourself.

The reason I recommended a week for this activity is that it will likely take you a couple of days to discover the negative patterns. Ask friends and family to help too! Once you discover these patterns, ask for help in correcting them (meaning when you accidentally use that negative phrase, friends and family make you aware of it or offer an alternative phrase). Again, it will take you several days (if not months) to make those changes.

160

While this kind of power depletion is subtle, it is so strongly patterned into our conscious and sub-conscious mind that it will totally undermine enchanted living if left uncorrected. Practice 43 (page 18) for enchanted living is that proactive, positive thoughts and words, lead to proactive, positive magick!

Readiness Means Movement

Understanding thought and word power brings us to movement. By definition, the word *movement* means not being at rest, or a course/process for transformation (note that this means a Warrior's thoughts are "not at rest" even if the body is!). Interestingly enough, movement can also relate to a specific theme in music; change the theme, and you change into a new movement! So what does this tell us about the Warrior?

First, it illustrates that movement works hand-in-hand with readiness. Because the Warrior is rarely "at rest" there is a sense of preparation, attentiveness, willingness, and availability that permeates this archetype. Second, it reveals that the Warrior is a force for change. When the Warrior's work is done, something will have transformed. This returns us to respect and erudition so that the Warrior's actions heal instead of harm.

Third, there is a kind of music and dance to the Warrior archetype. It's notable that many modern defense forms like Tai Chi look like an elaborate dance. Also, many fighters in professional fields like boxing take dance to help their motions become better coordinated and focused. So if one is to be a Warrior, first learn to dance!

Think about it for a minute. Dancing has a pattern. It responds to the energies of a specific moment with a physical expression, and it requires at least a little fitness. But to dance, one must be balanced (or you'll fall over). To respond, one must be ready.

Activity 6.3 - Sacred Dancing

There is a wonderful African saying: "If you can walk, you can dance." Nonetheless, the art of sacred dancing is a little different than a waltz or a night of boogying at a bar. Early humans regarded dance as indispensable to life's most important moments and to worship. This importance was relayed effectively by a New Guinea native in the 1800s. When asked by a visitor whether there was any "useless" dancing, his reply was, "No. Dances are never merely useless!"

In settings like this, and many others, dance was said to make spirits rejoice, honor the Divine, and put the dancer into communion with sacred energies. Some myths even say that sacred dance keeps the motion of the universe going! All of these things seem highly suited to the Warrior archetype, who often needs happiness to balance the difficulties of his or her tasks, who protects the children of the Divine, who wields sacred energies, and who is always in motion!

The most common accompaniment for sacred dancing was the drum (which you can make out of anything from an old coffee can to a bowl turned upside down). Find an implement that you can hold and drum, then stand still for a moment.

Breathe deeply. Listen to the rhythm of your breath and the beating of your heart. Begin to mirror that cadence on your drum. Focus on how the sounds combined make you feel. Blood's beating is part of the Warrior's call to action, to movement. Let your body move naturally to that meter. This is your personal rhythm and dance. Waltz with the God/dess and know yourself; know the Warrior. Make notes of your experience afterwards, especially any impressions you get about what this archetype means to you personally.

Finally, the aforementioned definitions show that, like both the Healer and Teacher, the Warrior becomes an instrument for personal change. The inner issues with which we all struggle become even more intense for a Warrior. Why? Because it seems that the Warrior's life is frequently a mirror of those things he or she wishes to overcome within. This is certainly challenging, but also rewarding. To know that the struggles with *being* the first part of the Wheel—being truthful, timely, connected, grounded, and whole—are those with which everyone struggles is somehow comforting. More importantly, the Warrior has the power to change those struggles into victory, not just for self, but for others.

Shamanic Focus: Presence and Attention

"There is not any present moment that is unconnected with some future one. The life of every man is a continued chain of incidents, each link of which hangs upon the former."

—Joseph Addison

163

Our concepts of rightness and wrongness often come down to shades of gray in everyday life. Like all of us, the Warrior is constantly barraged with this gray area and asked to make a choice. To help with this decision, the Warrior calls on the Healer's mindfulness, the Teacher's timing, and his or her own ability to be present and attentive.

Presence is a multidimensional way of living. In the first dimension, the Warrior has a specific presence, aurically, physically, and emotionally. Sensitives often feel a Warrior *before* they enter a room due to the charismatic energy the Warrior bears. A Warrior can use this presence to his or her advantage in several ways.

First, the strength and assurance of any person's character is perceptible on the astral level. When encountering or working with spiritual beings (or the astral presence of other people), either of whom may or may not have your best interests in mind, you want them to know who's the boss! Think of the television character Morticia Addams from *The Addams Family*, only with even more attitude projected into other dimensions, and you get the idea. Basically, you're trying to get other beings to think twice before messing with you!

Second, on a mundane level this presence helps with the role Warriors must assume. Warriors are often born leaders or very good followers. In the case of a leader, you want someone who has an assured, convincing demeanor and stance. That alone inspires confidence in others. In the case of a follower, you still have to convince the leader that your skills are up to snuff! In magick as in life, Practice 44 (page 18) is that a poised, positive bearing goes a long way toward making your case for you.

Despite all this outward expression of the Warrior's inner power, the Warrior can also mask this presence and simply not

164

be there (stealth spirituality, if you will) when necessary. This is a very important ability, and one that I wish I'd developed when I worked full time in an office setting. Here's an activity that will help you develop this skill.

Activity 6.4 - Invisibility

The root words for invisibility are translated as meaning "escaping sight." From the Warrior's perspective, this doesn't mean being absent, it simply means avoiding notice! To do this one must learn how to become indistinguishable from her surroundings; think of a chameleon with an attitude! The chameleon's skin tone shifts subtly to mimic the background setting so that when a human or other predators glance, they see nothing more than a harmless, unappetizing backdrop. This blending skill is what the Warrior needs to learn on an astral level for spiritual stealth.

Our auric and astral energies present a very specific image to those around us. You can't just simply delete those energies to avoid notice because then there's a huge hole where a person once was (which is very attention-getting!). If you don't believe me, put a whole bunch of similar items on a piece of white cloth or paper. Now, sit and look at them for a few minutes. Get to know how they appear and feel together. Next, take one away. There is now a noticeable gap in the pattern. From this activity, the Warrior learns that it is not enough to simply remove oneself from the surroundings. Instead, you have to mingle with them.

One way of accomplishing this is through a method called glamoury. Effectively, a glamoury puts on a specific spiritual atmosphere that mingles with your own to create a whole new portrait. For spiritual stealth, you will want that portrait to be reflect everything just as it's perceived by the person or situation from which you wish to remain invisible. Think of this like painting a picture with energy, then wrapping that picture around your personal auric and astral pattern.

A great place to practice this technique is at a crowded party. Sit somewhere comfortable and begin to see yourself as part of the furniture, the food, the glasses. In your mind's eye, let yourself simply melt into the surroundings. You'll know when you're doing this right because people will pay less and less attention to you, and may even seem surprised if they bump into your leg accidentally! You may also sense a shift in your aura that feels tingly or odd (as if you're not in your skin).

With time and practice, the Warrior can use this ability to quietly observe a situation before having to be called into action. This provides ample opportunity to measure a variety of perspectives, then make a wise decision based on those observations. If we could do this with all our actions in life, the outcomes would be much better. The Inner Warrior gives us the skill and inroad to begin so doing.

Now Is the Warrior's Theme

In the second dimension, the Warrior not only bears a specific presence but also *lives* presently, being wholly in this moment (per Practice 1, page 16). While he or she is aware of what led to this place and is likely pondering all the possible ramifications, *now* is the Warrior's theme. It is no coincidence that the word presence means attentive readiness, the Warrior's keynote! Rather than constantly mourning the past, the what-might-have-beens, the have-nots, or might-bes, the Warrior savors this moment knowing that attentiveness *now* can make or break any situation (per Practices 18 and 28, pages 17 and 18).

Besides having a direct correlation with readiness, presence and attention also influence the Warrior's power. If a person is trying to emulate the Warrior part of life's Wheel, he/she cannot give away power to unrealistic images and expectations of self, situations, others, or even the world. It is highly irresponsible to present or bear idealistic "perfect" images, because that breaks the rule of truth to self and undermines the trust that all archetypes are trying to cultivate. It is fine to be aware of these expectations and how they affect people, but do not give them too much undue attention.

Respect the Temple of Self

Now having said that, one of the images of the Warrior is a person who is mentally and physically fit. For some of us, this might not seem like a realistic goal. I would hazard to say, however, that working toward the Healer's wholeness is part of the Warrior's duty. This doesn't mean looking like a model, or having hulking muscles. What it does mean is tuning into the Warrior's sense of attention, in this case toward your own body, mind, and spirit. Practice 45 (page 19) for enchanted living is respect the temple of self; treat it as a sacred thing.

How? Quite simply, by taking the advice given by mothers and grandmothers everywhere! Eat well, get enough rest, feed your mind and spirit, and most of all, don't forget that you have needs too (per Practice 8, page 16). If you are not willing to do this, you cannot be an effective Warrior, and every quest you care deeply about will get done in a (if you'll forgive the expression) half-assed manner, if it gets done at all. The Healer's wholeness requires that we be our own best friend; the Teacher's timing requires that we recognize when to put down the sword and refill our inner well so we can live to fight another day.

Learning how to properly attend to self also helps in learning how to pay attention to others and situations. Attention means applying your mind to an object or idea and concentrating on it for a specific reason. During this moment of contemplation, other senses are on call to round out perceptions and gather information. Specifically, the eyes observe, the ears heed, the mind analyzes, but often the body is still. This stillness helps give your mind more energy with which to work, to attend to the matter at hand.

Nonmovement also provides the Warrior with that necessary pause for erudition, to internalize all the data being gathered. Better still, the Warrior's life is so filled with movement that even brief recesses are a welcome reprieve and an important chance to touch base with Spirit (Practice 16, page 17). Welcome these way stations and use them wisely.

THE EIGHT-FOLD PATH SPOTLIGHT: SPEECH AND ACTION

> *"Action springs not from thought, but from a readiness for responsibility."*
> —Dietrich Bonhoeffer

168

Good Warriors are good communicators. They inspire others to take up just causes by both word and deed. Proper speech recognizes that for communication to happen one must say what one means, and mean what one says. This, in turn, inspires right action, which we will talk about shortly. But it boils down to the fact that Warriors talk the talk and walk the walk. For people to follow confidently, there can be no dissonance between what the Warrior says and how he or she behaves.

For example, while a Warrior might wish to protect the Earth, he or she knows the means do not justify the ends. To illustrate: You wouldn't instruct others to blow up a building producing pollutants because that would harm what you're trying to heal (not to mention it being highly illegal!). That is also a very irresponsible use of power, something the Warrior doesn't take lightly. From this illustration, we can see that speech and action are intimately interconnected.

Right Speech

We are living in times when communication has reached new heights. In but a blink of an eye, we can get a message to someone halfway around the world. Nonetheless, communication has also reached new lows. An email cannot convey facial expression or subtle verbal cues. Even in our face-to-face dealings, we have forgotten how to talk to each other honestly. Overpopulation, crime, and other socioeconomic factors have caused people to retract into a space perceived as safe. Unfortunately, this space makes profound interaction nearly impossible, let alone enables other levels of interaction to be fully grasped. Each of us speaks from our space, our own truth, and we hear our own truth. We are not accustomed to speaking and listening from the other person's perspective because we don't put ourselves in that "space."

169

Right speech means saying things truthfully, but in a language or terms that the person hearing will comprehend. To do this, we have to be willing to walk a mile in someone else's shoes. A Christian, for example, will have great trouble accepting information about neo-pagan spirituality if the person communicating only uses neo-pagan jargon. Right speech for the parties involved in this fictitious conversation equates to finding a common ground, common vernacular, so both people in a conversation understand connotations rather than assuming meanings.

Right speech also means leaving harshness, exaggeration, embellishment, and gossip behind. Effectively, we must let our spirit's speak skillfully, and *not* our egos. Words are nothing more than thoughts spoken out loud, but this speech frequently needs a bit of editing before it reaches the audience! Thus, right speech returns to the Teacher's right thinking for assistance.

Learning the art of right speech, similar to everything else on the Sacred Wheel requires mindful practice, and also the awareness that what constitutes speech depends on both you and the intended audience. For example, letters can be a form of speech, as can both art and body positioning. Figuring out how to bring rightness into all of these dimensions isn't going to be an instantaneous accomplishment for anyone, even those gifted with good communication skills. When we write, or create, or speak, we must do so with our whole lives as a guide, knowing that whatever we convey in that moment will affect those around us.

Silence and Action

The Warrior's wisdom comes from knowing which words would be wasted on the audience, which words would harm, and, from the Healer/Teacher part of the Wheel, which words will instruct and create wholeness. In this respect, right speech can also mean right silence. There are times to verbalize, and times when those thoughts are best kept to ourselves.

Silence and stillness brings us to perfect action, which also, not surprisingly, sometimes means *not* acting. We talked at the beginning of this chapter about the Warrior pausing to evaluate before acting. This is a marvelous example of perfect action displayed by inaction, and power conservation all in one.

Right action is defined as promoting love, cultivating responsibility, safeguarding integrity, practicing generosity, transforming fear and confusion, and preventing harm. In pursuing this goal, the Warrior uses the thoughtfulness of Healer and the view of the Teacher. Thoughtfulness and perspective create the foundation for making a decision to act or remain still. One way of encouraging both is through the moving meditation.

Activity 6.5 - The Moving Meditation

For the purpose of this activity, meditation is defined as the act of stilling one's body and emotions, and being present in the moment complete with mindful breathing and contemplation as helpmates. This is the time to look at the true nature of things, but because the Warrior rarely sits still, he or she uses movement as part of the mediation process.

Begin as you might any meditation by centering and breathing evenly, but stay standing up. As you breath, gently whisper: Peace begins with me. When you feel so inclined, begin to walk. Don't rush

171

or worry about how your steps look, simply let yourself move purposefully. Change your mantra-like words to: I step for the good of all. Think about that motion as you say the words and move forward. Let the movement give energy to those words, your thoughts, and the reason for the meditation itself.

If at any point you feel yourself tensing up, stop and center again. The walking meditation must be comfortable and relaxed for it to be wholly effective. Practice the Healer's right diligence; do not be too loose, but also don't get so focused on walking that you lose right thinking. As Buddha might say: Do not try, simply do, and trust. If done correctly, any practice such as this results in joy, harmony, and personal transformation.

Right action relies on right speech, thinking, view, and livelihood for expression. Right action is aware of all the ways it touches on the whole path, and all that's contained therein. So you can begin to see how all parts of the Eight-Fold Path wrap around each other, support each other, and support the practitioner much as our Sacred Wheel keeps moving forward.

SENSORY CUE: HEARING

"From listening comes wisdom."

—Italian proverb

As a communicator, one of the things that Warriors learn to do is listen and really hear. This isn't just about superficials. There's a lot that goes on just above or below that to which most of us listen. Be it a conversation, the wind, or the movement of animals, we can learn how to hear very subtle messages and recognize omens by activating our Inner Warrior.

An effective Warrior must practice deep listening. This accomplishes much more than you might initially think. For example, a person who feels they are being ignored is much more likely to reach critical mass than someone who feels you're listening (and using the Warrior's attention). Here, right listening can defuse a potential bomb. In Eastern terms, this type of active listening relieves suffering: the pain of feeling insignificant, as if our ideas don't matter. Interestingly enough, this is also called "present listening," using the Warrior's skill.

To develop the Warrior's listening skills, the best thing you can do for yourself is relax and stop trying so hard. Instead, just accept the words into yourself even as the Earth soaks up a rain storm. Let each phrase and series of phrases settle into your being so that deep understanding can begin to form. If words only settle on your conscious mind, that is the only place you will relate to them. Similarly, if they only fall on your spirit, you will be missing the logical, conscious part of the equation. Present listening utilizes both the conscious and superconscious for interpretive insights.

As the Teacher speaks with love and the Healer touches with love, the Warrior listens with calmness and love. This encourages those speaking to open up completely, in ways they would not otherwise if listened to with criticism. Note that this approach doesn't just apply to people; it applies to situations. You know the saying, "If walls could talk"? Well, I happen to feel they can and *do* talk, but most of us aren't listening. Listening with serenity and patience is necessary to hearing everything in and around a situation, and being able to ponder that input for right action.

The Power of Silence

Because of this skill, the Warrior sitting alone in the woods is not alone. There is the sound of the wind in the

173

trees, the sound of the animals, the sound of his or her heart-beat moving in tune with the universe. In these moments, the Warrior refills the well of self and reconnects himself or herself with the All. This is how a Warrior also learns the power of silence. If we think back to right action, that in part encompassed stillness. Likewise, hearing also includes the void, a space where there is a pause between moments, between breaths, where nothing but profound, thundering silence exists. These are also often the moments when Spirit speaks because it does not have to fight so hard to get our attention.

What about a deaf person? Can he/she unleash the Inner Warrior through listening or silence? Of course! He can lip read, or hone his other senses to take the place of spiritual ears. Many hearing-impaired persons use touch and vibration in particular, which is interesting, because what we hear is due to our ears responding to a vibration. I only mention this because what we sometimes perceive as a person's limitations certainly aren't restrictive in the spiritual world. Practice 47 (page 19) for enchanted living is that there are no limits to magick and our spirits other than those we create. A person truly diligent about activating the archetypes won't be stopped by anything, be it the lack of eyes, legs, ears, or anything else.

MAGICKAL METHODS: CLAIMING POWER AND MANIFESTATION

> *"The principles you live by create the world you live in; if you change the principles you live by, you will change your world."*
>
> —Blaine Lee

I have always loved the bumper sticker that reads, "We are the people your mother warned you about." It makes me

174

laugh, but it also speaks to me of times when witches, wizards, and wise people were not laughed at, of times when spirituality worked hand-in-hand with daily life. While we might laugh at the old portraits of witches in black robes and hats riding on broomsticks, there was a certain power and presence evoked by that image, albeit negative. Part of the Warrior's task for himself or herself, and for the community he/she serves, is reclaiming the power and sanctity of the words *witch*, *shaman*, *seer*, *magick*, and other related terms (as well as the mental images those words evoke).

When mainstream religion grew to a place of influence, it recognized that the best way to dethrone the old ways, the ancestors, and the gods themselves, was to simply take away their power. The means to this end was deionizing, misrepresentation, or putting a new veneer on an old ritual or Being. The demonization is obvious in looking at Satan who, while having no bearing on metaphysical studies, is a direct rip-off of the horned god (the same god who represented humankind's link and responsibility to nature). The misrepresentation is painfully obvious during the witch hunts, and the new veneer can be seen in the list of saints who were once worshiped as god/desses in their own right by pagans (Bridgit comes immediately to mind).

Children of the Universe

Thankfully we are living in very different times, when the public image of non-mainstream spiritual traditions is changing. There is still plenty of work for the Warrior, however. He or she leads the forefront of the wave that moves out and reclaims our birthright. Practice 46 (page 19) for enchanted living states that we are children of the universe and people of power.

What is this power? It's magick. It's a miracle. It's the unleashed psychic potential within every human mind and soul. The Warrior reaches down deep, and upward to Spirit to reclaim, release, and guide that power. So can you.

I should warn you, however, that reclaiming power isn't just a brass ring that someone grabs, then afterwards rests comfortably on her laurels. The Warrior must accept responsibility for the way that power gets used. Of all the obligations of this archetype, this is perhaps the most important, not only on a personal level but also globally. We talked earlier about the Warrior being a force for change. The question is, what kind of change? Someone who wields power irresponsibly is likely to do more harm than good. He/she will tend to move to quickly, basing action on fear, partial truths, or personal desire, and the results can be downright disastrous.

Reclaiming Our Power

Speaking of results, exactly what happens when people reclaim and use their power effectively? Nothing less than manifestation. Manifest means making something real, plain, or evident. When the Warrior goes into action, filled with power, it is very real, living-in-the-moment, where the spiritual and mundane meet face-to-face. This is one time when Practice 49 (page 19) for enchanted living definitely bears out: Hard work is good magick.

The Warrior recognizes that there is a partnership between this world and the next, between soul and the Sacred. The Warrior's power begins within self and with Spirit, but for that power to flow out to the world in which we live, there's work involved. Everything from contemplation and planning to implementing a plan takes effort. That's what being an instrument for change, a co-creator means, and it's part of every archetype. When the Warrior's work is done, the purpose for movement will be quite plain. When the dust settles, the outcome becomes reasonably evident. And, if the Warrior acted with the archetypal lessons presented on the Wheel thus far, things will manifest for the good of all.

ELEMENTAL CORRESPONDENCE: FIRE

"The Path that leadeth on is lighted by one fire— the light of daring burning in the heart. The more one dares, the more he shall obtain."
—Helena Petrova Blavatsky

The awe and respect held in the communal heart toward Fire is nearly as old as humankind itself. In ancient times, our ancestors looked to the sun, which was worshiped as a god, and to the fire that warmed our bodies and food, and felt the two were connected. So much was the case that many societies consigned bodies to fire upon death to insure their safe journey back to god.

In metaphysical settings, Fire represents many things. It symbolizes passion, the beating of one's heart (e.g. the vital life force), purification, the banishment of darkness, and the hearth of a house, which is also the "heart" of a home, preserving the love within.

Fire and the Warrior's Duty

Now, let's apply this background and symbolism to the Warrior. First, it's interesting to note that it wasn't uncommon for solar gods and goddesses to also be those who presided over war, protection, and courage: three things that are part of this archetype. Prometheus might be the ultimate example of this, having become a hero to humankind by stealing Fire from the gods and teaching us how to use it!

Second, for hundreds of years, the gift of Fire was something worthy of protection because it was so sacred. Thus honoring and safeguarding Fire is a Warrior's duty, specifically the sacred Fire of the altar or the one around which the community gathers in worship. We see this potently displayed in the neo-pagan community, where firetenders gather a bit of coals from each gathering's central fire and keep it. That flame is returned and used to kindle the next fire. In this manner, symbolically the firetenders keep the warmth, love, and unity of the community "burning" in between the times when we can be together.

Third, while you're on the Warrior's part of the Sacred Wheel don't be surprised if you feel more passionate about everything. There is a depth of feeling to the Warrior archetype that even surpasses that of the Healer. This also makes it all the more difficult for the Warrior to put aside personal desires and emotions for the good of all. This is another reason Warriors deserve our respect, and a very good reason that our communities should give Warriors as much support and protection as they do us (something that seems to often be neglected).

The Burning of a Warrior's Heart

Fourth, the rhythm of one's heart is something the Warrior often uses to center and connect with his or her inner source of power. Life's fiery essence exists in that sound and cadence. The admonition for the Warrior is to not leave those inner Fires unattended or let them get overstoked. The unattended fire can come out in explosions or die altogether. The overstoked fire burns, quite harshly, often in the form of unproductive anger.

178

Finally, with regard to purifying, banishing darkness, and protecting love in the home, these all certainly qualify as part of the Warrior's tasks. A Warrior strives to purify a wrong or transform the darkness into light each time he or she undertakes a fight for the greater good. And most importantly, a Warrior safeguards the home, which is a sacred space in which love and spirituality are nurtured side by side. In the burning of the hearth fire, one may see the burning of a Warrior's heart.

As an aside, divination by Fire is one of the more traditional methods of fortune telling, and it might be an ideal method for the Warrior to cultivate to assist with attention and hearing skills. This method of divining uses both the eyes and ears for interpretive values, so it can improve the keenness of both senses. If you'd like to try this yourself, here's an activity to help.

Activity 6.6 - Fire Scrying

First, you will need a fire source. A candle is fine, but a larger fire (outside or in) tends to work a little better for the audio effects. If possible, light the fire using a non-chemical source. Once it's burning steadily, sit down in front of the fire and settle your mind and spirit. Breathe deeply and evenly as you would for any meditation. Listen to that breath and the beating of your heart and let it lead you to another level of awareness. Focus your eyes on the fire, but if your vision begins to blur, let it. That's exactly what needs to happen.

If you have a specific question, it helps to keep that question in your mind as you watch, but the spirits of Fire tend to be rather independent.

They'll show you what they think you need to see! Sometimes you will receive actual images formed by the flames. Other times you simply have to interpret the behavior and sounds of the flames. Here is a list of some of the traditional correspondences associated with Fire's movement and sounds:

* Crackling or sparking: news is coming (often good).

* Soot falling around the fire: An important message will arrive soon. Look at the pattern of the soot for more insights.

* Sizzling: Arguments or anger getting in the way of positive resolution.

* Blue flames: spirits are influencing this situation or guiding spirits (ancestors) are trying to tell you something.

* Tall flames: Good thoughts or wishes directed toward you or the situation in question.

* Sudden blazing: A stranger (or distant acquaintance) is somehow involved in this question.

* Smokey fire: dissention and disagreement is the root of the problem, and it's covering up an obvious solution.

    Alternatively, this indicates magickal or psychic influences (usually negative ones).

* Spitting fire: Someone in a leadership position (or who considers themselves to be so) is irate.

* Flames moving to the right: Generally a "yes" answer.

* Flames moving to the left: Generally a "no" answer.

Beyond these generalized interpretations, don't forget to open your other senses. Use the Healer's sense of smell and if you catch an aroma on the wind, consider what it means. Similarly use the Teacher's sense of taste and see what the fire puts into the wind in the way of flavors. All of these cues together can give you a lot of information with which to work.

One last reflection with regard to Fire. Consider the tale of the great firebird, the phoenix. According to Egyptian mythology, every 500 years this creature built a nest of flaming myrrh in the temple of Ra and burned to death in it. From those ashes a reborn phoenix rises, young and whole, to return to Arabia, its home. This reveals that a Warrior is tempered by the Fires he or she endures and is actually strengthened and renewed by them in the end. There are literally dozens of ancient myths and legends that tell of a Warrior's battle with Fire, be it a fire-breathing dragon, a lake of fire, fire gini, maddening fires, or a plethora of other literally heated challenges. This cycle of trial by Fire has not stopped for spiritual soldiers, and you must be prepared for the flame.

The Warrior cycle of the Wheel often includes a lot of upheaval and battles from which to choose. Don't be deterred by this seeming chaos, for it has a purpose and your energy. Look to the Fire within and the Fires of Spirit to sustain your conviction and power. When the battle is over, you might be weary, but you will find that it has provided valuable experiences on which to draw in the future, not to mention a healthy dose of wisdom.

SACRED DUTY: OFFERING

*"The only gift is a portion of thyself. . . the poet
brings his poem; the shepherd his lamb. . ."*
—Ralph Waldo Emerson

People frequently ask me why I spend so much time looking at the definitions of various words in my writings. In part, it's because I feel that the spiritual application for a word, and the mundane meaning are often quite different. Additionally, by looking at the roots of a word, we can begin to understand what our ancestors really meant. This is true with the word *offering.*

By standard dictionary definition, offering means to bring forward for consideration. Alternatively, it's defined as presenting something as an act of worship, as a confirmation, a service, or a sacrifice. It also means to be "at hand."

Using this definition as a starting point, let's examine why the duty of offering is important to the Warrior. First, part of the Warrior's duty is to make peace or bring resolution wherever possible. That means he or she must know how to bring forward sound strategy and methodologies that everyone can consider. In this respect, the Warrior is as much a diplomat as a fighter!

Next, Warriors were often known for giving an offering or sacrifice before they went into service. This release to the Powers was a plea for protection and blessing. It also reflected the Warrior's desire to confirm that his or her efforts were, indeed, for the good of all. Just because a Warrior is confident, doesn't mean being foolhardy. We are all human, and prone to human error. The spiritual Warrior needs divine guidance and blessing so that the sword he wields is used in the best possible manner.

For example, periodically my family has an urgent financial need, which is something that brings out my protective Warrior nature. At this juncture, I look at things that I cherish like special pieces of jewelry, nice crystals, statuary, or anything else that I personally purchased and consider a treasure. From those items, I pick one to become my offering by putting it up for sale (giving to receive). Each time I have done this, the minute the item sold, other unexpected monies also came into our hands through a job contract, a refund of some kind, and so forth.

Now, I know that sounds very foreign to some readers, but that is how offerings work. I know that I can't always see how Spirit can and will provide, but I can open the way for those blessings. In the process, however, I also remain a participant and co-creator by giving up something I care about, for something I love even more (my family). It's very good magick.

Offering One's Self

Looking to the third definition, being "at hand" returns us to our keyword of readiness. The Warrior must always be ready to make an offering, even if that means laying down his or her life for a greater good. That is an extreme example, but it is part of the Warrior's quarter of the Wheel. Symbolic or literal death is part of life, and it's a part that the Warrior must embrace as passionately as all other aspects thus far. I pray our spiritual soldiers never have to give as much as their ancestors for our freedom, but unless we tend our freedoms daily, it could come down to that kind of battle.

On a less intense level, offering oneself can also mean offering personal time, especially to a task you generally avoid. Personal time is often very scarce and valuable to the Warrior. Giving up a bit of that is no small gesture. Indeed, at each juncture on the Wheel, we are called again to service. The question then becomes whether or not we answer, and if we answer, exactly how. Offerings are one way of not only saying yes, but serving with a glad heart.

CONCLUSION

At the end of the day and the end of the battle, when all is said and done, the Warrior rests. As she looks up from weary eyes, she beholds something new. The fight is over. The past life is over. Now is time for rebirth, for a new vision. Now once again the Wheel turns, and the Visionary is born.

Chapter 7

The Visionary

"Whither is fled the Visionary gleam/ Where is it now, the glory and the dream."
—William Wordsworth

Our Sacred Wheel has come full circle. In the last quarter of this quest we find the archetype of the Visionary. A Visionary is someone who sees what many of us cannot (or will not) see. Thus, the people embracing this archetype are among the most misunderstood, censured, and persecuted. With this in mind, it is no wonder that this part of our trek is the last spoke on the Wheel; it is the most difficult.

Thankfully, the Visionary doesn't reach this place without a lot of incredible moments held tightly to his or her heart like a shield. The Healer's moments taught patience and the way of wholeness. The Teacher's moments taught us to stay connected and remember who we are in our soul of souls. The Warrior's moments taught us both action and stillness.

These lessons become the Visionary's tool kit. When you are misinterpreted, composure is a great ally. When you know and trust yourself, it is much easier to handle rejection or misrepresentation. Finally, when you know when to act, and when to remain still, you can avoid a whole lot of misunderstanding.

Now the 49 practices of the previous archetypes come together to sustain and support the Visionary. In fact, this chapter will only have one practice, which is simply to live the other 49 and be yourself. You are a wholly important spiritual being and have a great deal to offer the world, including a new vision, if you just allow it, if you simply will trust and *be*.

Seeking Truth

Now, knowing this doesn't lessen the struggles that come along the way, nor does it change the somewhat lonely nature of the Visionary's work. The image of the gurus and monks who retreat to solitude didn't come about by happenstance. The Visionary needs regular quiet and isolation to look within and to Spirit to gather his or her gospel (for lack of a better word). But that's not the only reason this part of the Wheel is difficult and solitary on a regular basis.

Why then? Well, first the Visionary seeks after core truth and then shares those ideas with others. Sadly, there aren't a lot of people who really want to hear the truth. If you don't think this is so, just listen to our everyday conversations. When people ask one another, "How are you?" do they really want to know the whole truth? (You know the stuff about kids with colds, unemployment, the broken refrigerator, and so on.) No. The question is simply a social convention.

An Instrument of Change

A majority of human actions and interactions, even spiritual ones, have that superficial quality, and there seems to be a lot of resistance to changing that. The Visionary encounters

188

that resistance daily simply by being who and what he/she is. To paraphrase the wisdom of Gandhi, for the Visionary his or her life *is* the message. He/she is the instrument of change.

Second, the Visionary stresses the need for each of us to hold tightly to our higher purpose in this life. Nonetheless, it's kind of tough to hold onto something that you have not found. To discover purpose requires nothing less than intense digging into the darkest part of ourselves, shining light there, and then examining ourselves truthfully (per Practice 6, page 16). I know of no one for whom this is effortless or comfortable, and it's easy to vent that discomfort on the messenger who handed you that darn shovel in the first place.

Third, the Visionary is a powerful dreamer who likewise tells us to dare to dream. More importantly, he or she says: Dare to make those dreams come true! In an overpopulated world where it seems one voice gets wholly lost in the throng, it's easy to stop hoping and dreaming. This is a terrible tragedy. When people lose that, they also lose their magick and power, giving it over to apathy, the "what-might-have-beens," or pessimism. In the face of this darkness, this optimistic Visionary tells us that there is another, bright, substantial way to live and see the world. They call us with this message: Open the eyes of your souls, let the light in, and believe once more.

KEYNOTE: UNDERSTANDING AND PERSPECTIVE

> *"Humor is perhaps a sense of intellectual perspective: an awareness that some things are really important, others not; and that the two kinds are most oddly jumbled in everyday affairs."*
>
> —Christopher Morley

To uncover, understand, and convey truth, the Visionary must remain open. While Visionaries often have a feel for where they're going, the vision must guide and direct the destination. This makes this part of the Wheel the most intuitive of all, and the one requiring the most trust.

Consider for a moment what it is like to live without any fixed perspectives. Blue is no longer blue. It is a color called blue but that construct could change as new information, a new vision, comes to you. This can be very disconcerting, yet the Visionary accepts it as part of the job description and simply trusts (per Practices 4 and 35, pages 16 and 18). Is it any wonder a lot of Visionaries are considered odd by societal standards?

Also consider what it is like to be your own Visionary. Just like the Healer had to heal self, the Teacher had to teach self, and the Warrior had to protect and fight for self, the Visionary is called to *see* for self. In other words, rather than looking outwardly to others for insights, the Visionary must be willing to listen to that small voice within. After all, if the Visionary isn't ready to accept and integrate new perspectives, why should anyone listen to him (per Practice 24, page 17)?

In this respect, the Visionary has mastered Practices 19 and 25 (page 17). He or she has accepted the priest/ess position in personal matters. He or she has also taken a long hard look at the remainder of the Wheel's road and what it's taught (e.g. understanding). Now the time comes to turn that vision outward and forward. The tool for this part of the job is having a unique perspective.

The Visionary's perspective of the world is wholly different and often quite childlike in its wonder. Do you remember what it was like to look at a dandelion for hours and be wholly engrossed in its beauty? What about the pure joy in blowing that flower's seeds to the four winds? This is the outlook a Visionary bears, but with greater wisdom and a stronger connection to Spirit.

Activity 7.1 - A Walk on the Wild Side

For this activity, you should give yourself at least a full hour in a private, natural location (preferably one where you find peace and inspiration). The day before you go, make sure to get plenty of rest, and just prior to leaving take a few moments to ground, center, and speak to Spirit. Ask for divine guidance in seeing things a little differently today, seeing things with the Visionary's perspective.

When you arrive, make yourself as comfortable as possible. Physical uneasiness makes broadened perception more difficult. Also, try to set aside any preconceived notions of what to expect. This archetype is like the others; let it out of the box (per Practice 31, page 18) to become whatever it's meant to be in your life.

Once you're comfortable, close your eyes for a few minutes and open all your senses (see Chapter 2 for ideas). Let your aura reach out to the surroundings and mingle with all the energies there: the wash of a dew drop, the whispers of wind, the warm sun on your back, and the cool ground beneath your feet. Now, slowly open your eyes. Don't look anywhere in particular. Just wait until something strikes you.

When your eyes or other senses draw you to something specific, consider how many times you've seen that very object or animal, or experienced something similar. What's different about this moment, this experience? What truth, what dream, what vision can you carry from this moment out into the real world? When you answer that question and know the answer to be genuine, you have taken the first giant step down the Visionary's path.

Reaching Truth

By the way, it's not necessary to run and find someone to share this vision with right away. In fact, the perspective offered by this archetype is meant for you at first. Let what you've just experienced settle into your soul. Think of it like a seed of knowledge. When you sense a small sprout growing, continue to wait. When that seed blossoms into fullness in *you*, then it's time to share it with others, because now you see the whole lesson, not just the seed's outer shell.

This is perhaps the hardest lesson for the Visionary. It's easy to get excited about something fresh and inspiring, but we have to remember to digest that seed's hull first. Beneath the surface of that initial vision, there are many other layers of spiritual perspective to ponder before you reach truth. And just like the petals of a flower, each one that unfolds gives us a better picture of how that truth will manifest when fully grown, both within and without.

Now at first this waiting seems to break Practice 38 (page 18), applying our knowledge, but it doesn't. Instead, the Visionary tarries long enough to be responsible with and to the perspective he or she has been given. It is a true spiritual treasure, and therefore the Visionary treats it with due respect. This, in turn, honors self and Spirit, who are cooperative partners in the Visionary business. Our souls have the potential to reach beyond this physical shell and glimpse the eternal light. Is it any wonder that there are so many myths about great hero's receiving a vision in a blinding flash? Spirit is the spark of that flame!

SHAMANIC FOCUS: SILENCE, TRUTH, REALNESS

> *"Silence is a sounding thing/ To one who listens hungrily."*
> —Gwendolyn Bennett

An Ute prayer says in simple beauty: Earth, teach me stillness. This is also the Visionary's prayer, for in stillness Spirit speaks. In stillness, dream appears. In stillness the vision becomes. Where the Warrior was nearly always on the move spiritually, the Visionary seeks the quite soulfulness in which to remain open and receive. This is actually a good approach to remember at any juncture on the Sacred Wheel.

Silence and Truth

Think for a moment of how all types of sounds barrage our every waking and sleeping moments. Honking horns, airplanes flying overhead, boom boxes played at maximum volume: It's really amazing that anyone can think straight, let alone find inspiration with all that chaos. Add to this assault the Warrior's goal of attentiveness, the Healer's goal of thoughtfulness, and the Teacher's goal of connectedness. Each of these things requires a kind of slowing down, a soulful hush that isn't common in the 9-5 world. Nonetheless, that very quiet, that very purposeful pace, is exactly what starts activating and energizing the Inner Visionary.

Not coincidentally, this is also the womb from which truthfulness and realness are born. Humans strive to convince others of their rightness because it's much more comfortable than to admit we might be wrong, especially in matters of faith. Nonetheless, the Inner Visionary expects more of us than that. Truthfulness requires that we sacrifice that comfort for a greater good: enlightenment. Realness requires that we go about that sacrifice in a manner that is wholly true to self (akin to the Warrior's offering).

To be truthful means letting down walls, which is also part of the Visionary's openness. Truthfulness develops two-way communications between self and soul, between self and others, between self and Spirit. And truthfulness remains wholly responsible to our words and actions (per Practice 32, page 18), starting with sharing only those visions that we've truly integrated and *live*.

Activity 7.2 - Truth or Dare

Those of you who have seen the movie *Liar, Liar* know that watching someone who is accustom to coloring the truth suddenly speak honestly can be both amusing and shocking. Truth surprises people. It sets them off guard and takes a while to digest before everything gets back in balance. This exercise will give you a chance to see the effects of truthfulness for one full day.

It doesn't matter what day, but vow to tell the truth for one 24-hour period. Take a notebook with you to record your experiences and their results. As you manifest truth, take care to use the abilities you've gathered from other parts of the Wheel. Apply the Healer's right diligence, the Teacher's right thinking, the Warrior's right speech, and the mind of perfect love. Truth can be gentle, constructive, enlightening, and motivational, but if delivered without those five faculties, it can become harsh, cutting, caustic, and destructive. See what a day of truth produces in your life and the lives of those around you.

Realness

Truthfulness and realness work hand-in-hand. You can't be honest if you're not real. The best way I know of to explain realness comes from my own life. As a writer, I've found that some people put me on a pedestal or have unrealistic notions of what my day-to-day life is like (having images of glamour, popularity, and wealth). Now, if you were to visit my home you'd quickly see that simply isn't the case. I scrub my floors by hand, have children constantly messing up the house, mow the lawn, and so on. In other words, I am the proverbial "girl next door." Nothing odd or unique, except that I happen to write for a living.

When I go on the road, I make sure that "the girl next door" is exactly what people see. There is no flash and fanfare, no high-horse attitudes, just me. I want to be real with my readers. I want them to know me for all my attributes and all my faults. Otherwise it's easy to have unrealistic expectations not only of me, but also of those expectations they apply for themselves. Now, it's good to have goals and hopes, but they need to be balanced with a healthy dose of common sense, that is, realism!

Another good example of realness was illustrated in the *Velveteen Rabbit*. Here, the well-loved bunny and its companions wonder what it's like to be real. Through this charming story, Margery Williams does a fantastic job of showing us that realness is about *being* who we are. It's about self-awareness and expressing self in the most positive way possible: uplifting those things that make us unique and accomplished, and working on those things that hold us back.

Have you ever noticed how elderly people often just say what they mean without embellishment and do what they want even if it isn't social convention? That's because they have already lived through the years when they felt they had to conform to one image or another. Now the time has come for realness, for enjoying who they are fully.

One would hope that we could learn this lesson earlier in life so that, alongside truthfulness, it could begin to release a Visionary who is genuine in word, deed, and perspectives. Do, however, be patient with yourself. It takes practice and diligence to begin living in truth and realness, and you're bound to falter from time to time. The Inner Visionary recognizes that we still have human failings and inherent habits that derail our quest to fulfill the Wheel. He or she also sees beyond those limits, knowing we can still succeed. Keep trying!

THE EIGHT-FOLD PATH SPOTLIGHT: MINDFULNESS AND CONCENTRATION

> *"Success in life is a matter not so much of talent as of concentration and perseverance."*
> —C. W. Wendte

In Eastern tradition, the lesson of mindfulness is considered the pulse of Buddha's wisdom. Quite simply, if one is mindful, all other aspects of the Eight-Fold Path fall into place, as do the points of the Sacred Wheel. Effectively, not only does mindfulness cultivate the Inner Visionary, but it also supports the process of enlightenment.

Mindfulness includes things like attention. It also includes the mind of perfect love that we talked about earlier in this book. If you think of this word in hyphenated form for a moment (mind-fullness), it becomes easier to comprehend what Buddha was trying to say. In part the question becomes: What fills our minds? Are we feeding our minds good soul food? Are we filling our thoughts with uplifting, loving views? Do we allow negatives or impractical notions to sneak in and rob us of truthfulness and realness? These are not easy questions but they beg our consideration.

It's very interesting to review the word *mindfulness* as it appears in some of the older writings. In Sanskrit, it means "remember," which to me indicates that mindfulness reminds us of the Warrior's lesson, namely our role as spiritual people, as people of power. Remembering also has to do with the ancestors, with those who have come before us, and what their successes and failures taught us about the human soul and spirit.

Activity 7.3 - Ancestral Tree

For this activity, begin doing some research on your family tree. Take the names of at least three people in your family line whom you find interesting and learn as much about their lives as you can (or the era in which they lived if you can't get more personal information).

When you're done gathering data, go to your altar or another sacred space and light a candle to honor the spirits of those people. Say a brief prayer, asking for insight into what you're about to read over. Then review the notes. Is there something you can glean there? A tidbit of inspiration or wisdom?

For example, I did this with my grandmother because I still had strong memories of her. In reviewing my notes, I realized she epitomized a Victorian lady. She was always proper, knew how to run an efficient and immaculate home, and could cook up a storm. Nonetheless, despite this construct, she mindfully found time for laughter, for picking huckleberries with us as children and making them into muffins at the crack of dawn just to roust us out of bed.

My lesson in this was that being organized and competent did not mean having to lose my joy. If anything, it should give me more time to be playful and enjoy the special people in my life.

I believe each of us can discover similar wisdom and lessons in our family units. Remember: Those who do not remember history and learn from it are often doomed to repeat it! This is certainly not the goal of right mindfulness.

In Chinese, the word for mindfulness roughly translates as "now heart." What a powerful image! Being present and fully in the moment (per Practice 1, page 16), with the mind of love as a guide, allows the Inner Visionary to blossom in amazing ways. There is an intensity to this approach to life, a depth, that few of us touch unless we really apply ourselves. In these moments, we see things multidimensionally, we see them fully, we see with the eyes of realness, the eyes of a Visionary. This in turn inspires appreciation. We begin to treasure the whole of life's network as precious because we are mindful of what it means. More importantly, we treasure each other as precious, knowing that we need each other.

Associated Actions of Mindfulness

It is said that mindfulness has four associated actions. The first is to simply stop (the Warrior's pause). Second is to calm yourself. This keeps mindfulness from being colored by the heat of a moment. Third is to rest. By rest I don't mean sleep, but instead balance yourself. Be in the moment, be centered, and remain at ease with your environment. Finally, mindfulness requires healing. A lot of our ways of thinking have been diseased by circumstances, or by being untrue. Those ways must heal before we can be truly mindful.

Additionally, mindfulness heals others. Just as we learned in the Healer archetype, once you are whole within, it begins to naturally affect the without. Consider how important another person feels when you attend to him or her mindfully. That sense of worth, of being loved, is a miracle, and it will work wonders. Even more so, you not only attend them, but *see* them, understand them. So many people suffer from feeling misunderstood. Mindfulness toward these lost souls acts like a healing salve. It transforms that sense of being lost, and replaces it with a vision-driven awareness of place and worth.

Focal Points of Mindfulness

Mindfulness also has four established focal points. The first is toward our body. How many of us dislike the way we look? We complain about an inch of fat here, a wrinkle or gray hair there. We constantly compare ourselves to unrealistic media images of what is beautiful and then wonder why we're not happy. We are not being truthful, real, or mindful toward our bodies. At some point in our life, in order to be fully mindful, we also have to make peace with our physicality. Your body is the temple of your soul. Honor it accordingly.

The second focal point is our emotions. Feelings shouldn't be separate from the rest of spiritual awareness, nor should they be wholly motivated by externals. When you live in the moment, you feel the moment. Don't cling to that feeling,

199

nor reject it; simply recognize it, greet it, then let it be. Embracing your feelings with mindfulness gives you more control over how you express those feelings. This is very important for Visionaries, because the vision can be a highly emotional experience.

To give you an example, perhaps some insight came as to the cause of a problem, and it left the Inner Visionary feeling very angry toward that source. Mindfulness instructs that rather than letting anger rule you, you embrace it and get past it. This allows the energy to become an instrument of change by asking yourself what has made you angry. How do you change that situation? Get up and do just that using all the other aspects of the Path and the Wheel to guide that Warrior's action.

The third focus of mindfulness is, not surprisingly, the mind. Humans have a natural tendency to scatter their thoughts. By so doing, they lose a lot of power and often get distracted from what's in this moment. Additionally, we aren't always fully aware of how one thought leads to another, sometimes with very negative results. While regretting harm done to another is a good thought, if you cling to that it turns into guilt, which is nonproductive (and also a waste of power). Mindfulness asks us to stay focused, and rather than allowing thoughts to become unwholesome, we either turn them around or act on them!

Now it's normal to have agitated, jealous, or angry feelings, or to experience other forms of mental distraction. The key here is recognizing when this is happening. We don't pay attention to what we're thinking, and that is not mindfulness. You can't change those things of which you're not aware until it's too late! Just as we have to embrace emotions, we should embrace our thoughts and become responsible toward them.

The mindful focus towards the mind works hand-in-hand with the fourth focus: objects and perspective. Our mind is like a stage. When we direct our attention to someone or something, that person, place, or thing becomes the object of our perception. Once something or someone is on that stage, we must allow the Teacher's right view and thinking to take over. We can also apply the Visionary's own talent for seeing things differently so that the realness of what we're seeing comes into our thoughts. This is exactly where right concentration comes into the picture!

Concentration Encourages Right Action

Right concentration is a kind of symmetry where both the ongoing activeness of the mind, and those objects/people of selective focus, are honored. Think of this like an image and a setting. Before you is the selective focus, but the background is still present and both are important. By remaining aware of both, we encourage the Warrior's right action, too.

Another important part of concentration comes with meditation. Being in the moment, becoming the moment, turning our thoughts inward to better understand the without: This is meditation and right concentration. Within the mind, there are no limits but those we create for ourselves. Consciousness need not be constrained, nor should vision. Meditation is the tool used to release consciousness and vision from material constructs to touch the eternal.

During mindful concentration like this the ancient phrase, "I am," has great meaning. Just as a wave is already water, you are in self, and you are also All. There is nothing separating you from anything else. The distance between here and eternity is but a thought. We need not physically travel to experience a sense of place, but for that kind of miracle to happen our focus, our concentration, our perception must be wholly right and activated by the Visionary within. If we are living the Eight-Fold Path and honoring our Wheel, that rightness will come naturally.

Sensory Cue: Vision

"Where there is no vision, there is no hope."
—George Washington Carver

It is interesting that in various languages, the wise people were often called seers. No one who used this kind of terminology was talking about physical eyesight. They instead talked of an ability that goes in many directions and many dimensions to touch on those things of starlight and dreams. In other words, the Inner Visionary cannot depend on what the body perceives visually for their sight; they must depend on the eyes of Spirit.

Individuals gifted with this unique sight were often the fortunetellers and diviners of their town or village (which equates to a type of counseling service too). People would go to this wise person asking about love, crops, husbandry problems, and all other manner of common needs, hoping to tap into that wondrous vision of the seer for guidance. Truthfully, little has changed in modern times.

Even with all our technological advances, most people have at least a little curiosity about the future, let alone the energies that are shaping this very moment. This is one of the roles a Visionary can fill fairly easily, and without some of the traditional skepticism. After all, most folks who go to a diviner do so because they already have some trust in the system, or are at least open enough to be curious. Such a reception is welcome to the Visionary, and it's a great arena in which to practice and hone the abilities of this archetype.

202

Divinatory Tools

If you feel you'd like to try one or more divinatory tools as a means of touching and manifesting your Inner Visionary, I'd like to issue some precautions. First, bear in mind that the future is constantly shifting and changing. What you "see" in any tool at one reading can change come the next, because we are people with free will and everything that happens between those readings can change the future.

When you use a divinatory tool, treat it respectfully. Give yourself quiet time to reflect on the symbolism before you, and honestly consider if you're in the right frame of mind to receive insights. For example, if you're depressed about not finding a new job, this probably isn't the best time to try and do a reading for yourself because you'll tend to see only the worst. That's simply the way our emotions color the interpretation of symbolic material.

Similarly, if you're tired or out of sorts, it's not the best time to read for anyone else either! A wise Visionary must be able to use the Warrior's awareness of when to act, and when to bow out gracefully. I only mention this because people will naturally be drawn to the Visionary's talent for seeing. You must be ready, willing, and able to say no especially if you see people depending more on that reading than on their own inner voice and Spirit.

Beyond those simple guidelines, here's a brief list of do's and don'ts for divination that you may find helpful:

DO:

* Try several different tools until you discover which one works best for you.
* Consider setting up your reading area like a sacred space to improve the overall atmosphere and sensual cues with which you have to work.

* Be specific (or have the person asking the question be specific in forming that thought silently).

* Find the right tool for the right job. A yes-or-no system (like coin flipping) won't give you many details.

* Remember that some questions will not have pat answers, if you get any insights whatsoever. Sometimes the future is too convoluted to get a solid vision.

* Be kind and gentle even when delivering bad news. The rule of "Do unto others…" is a good one to follow in the way you relate divinatory information.

* Remind yourself or the person for whom you're reading that what divination provides is insight, not carved-in-stone missives. They (or you) must choose how to apply that "truth" to daily living and the situation at hand.

* Make notes about each reading and read them over periodically to gauge your accuracy. Like most spiritual arts, practice makes perfect!

DO NOT:

* Read for anyone toward whom you cannot put aside personal feelings or desires. The Visionary must be willing to leave ego out of the picture to truly see for another person (or whole communities).

* Read when you're rushed for time, sick, angry, or otherwise negatively influenced.

* Let others volunteer your gifts or you'll become like a side show act. Use the Teacher's timing to

know the best moment and/or situation in which to offer those gifts.

* Seek out symbolic or literal spiritual meaning where none is necessary (not everything in life has to have deep, soulful significance).

* Seek out an answer just based on the question posed. Spirit often uses a divinatory session to speak about other important matters that have remained unspoken.

If you follow this list, keeping Spirit as a co-pilot in your quest for vision and understanding, the outcomes are bound to be much more successful and life affirming.

MAGICKAL METHODS: RITUAL AND ASTRAL JOURNEYING

"The journey is the reward."

—Taoist saying

Our lives are a ritual. Everyday we follow comfortable routines that add coherency to our lives. While spiritual rituals are a little different in form and purpose as other ones in our life, they are equally (if not more) important.

The Visionary uses ritual for a variety of reasons. First, the act of creating sacred space provides an ambiance more conducive to receiving insight. Sacred space keeps unwanted energies neatly outside and erases the traditional boundaries of time and space.

Second, ritual builds energy that's directed at a specific goal. For the Visionary, this goal is typically rooting out the truth of a matter. Perhaps even more importantly, the words and actions of ritual transform thoughts, turning them away from the mundane and toward the spiritual. So now the Visionary's inner "ambiance" matches that of the sacred space around him or her.

Third, and most importantly to this archetype, ritual supports a connection with Spirit. Here, at the altar, a candle burns brightly or some other symbol sets, welcoming Spirit into the space. Once that door is opened, communion may ensue. In this manner, ritual consummates the relationship between Visionary and the Divine so that he or she can better fulfill their duties.

Vision Quest

It's interesting that the word *ritual* means "fit together." The Visionary within each of us attempts to do just that: fit together small tidbits of awareness into greater truths. These pieces are the patterns of power (see also Chapter 1) that span the universe. Without that "fitting together," we cannot hope to progress as spiritual people. That's where ritual and the vision quest become connected.

A vision quest is exactly as it sounds: a personal journey, the goal of which is not simply awakening the Inner Visionary, but also empowering him or her! In the state of heightened awareness that a vision quest brings, gathering insights becomes much easier (and the depth of those insights is far more dramatic).

Activity 7.4 - The Vision Quest

Choose a safe location for your vision quest, one where you know the lay of the land or where you can have someone check on you. Before the quest, practice trance work. Specifically work on combining meditation, chanting, and breath so that your levels of meditation become deeper and deeper. The day prior to the quest, fast if it's physically feasible, and get plenty of rest. Just prior to setting out to the location, take a slow ritual bath in which you cleanse away negativity and worldly energy and turn your mind and spirit toward the task at hand.

As you approach the designated location for your vision quest (which, by the way, can last several hours or several days depending on your constraints, but it's best to have an open-ended time frame) think of it like a church. Create sacred space in a ritualistic manner suitable to your Path (such as calling the four Quarters in Wicca or through smudging and chanting in Native traditions).

Now get comfortable and begin to meditate. You'll know you're reaching the right level of awareness when you feel somewhat light and tingly (like just before you go to sleep). At some juncture, you'll begin to experience something; exactly what that something is depends much on the individual. Many questers tell of a dream-like world with a specific entryway and exit, through which they travel and learn. While the tapestry in between entry and exit may change from quest to quest, these two symbolic doors seem to remain fixed like landmarks.

Exactly what you gather on such an important spiritual journey is also very personal. You may come to better understand your life's purpose or this juncture on the Wheel. You may discover your medicine—a kind of attentive vigilance that overcomes barriers and manifests wholeness. Or you may come away with seemingly nothing at all, only to discover the lessons in the quest days or months later. No matter what happens, don't be discouraged. Simply trust that the effort itself begins unlocking your Inner Visionary and all the perceptions that archetype needs to succeed.

By the way, a quest need not be a once-in-a-lifetime thing. By definition, quest means to seek out or inquire. By this definition, the Visionary qualifies as questing throughout his or her portion of the Sacred Wheel. After all, it is his or her job to reach beyond normal perception for greater perspectives that can change the human condition individually or globally.

This reaching compels diligent pursuit and questioning, not just of self and the world, but also of Spirit. In other words, it compels ritual, truthfulness, realness, mindfulness, and concentration — all the other characteristics the Visionary hopes to develop before the Wheel turns again. In ritual, he or she connects with Spirit. Through truthfulness and realness, he or she rediscovers self-assurance, and begins to trust in the Visions received from Spirit. And with mindful concentration, all life becomes the ritual, the act of worship, in which a person can receive divine guidance and wisdom, anytime, anywhere.

ELEMENTAL CORRESPONDENCE: AIR

"There is a great wind is blowing, and that gives you either imagination or a headache."

—Catherine the Great

In magickal traditions, the Air element is characterized as having motivational, transformational, and inspirational energy. More directly influencing the Visionary, this is the Element of intangibles including psychism, which are so much a part of the Visionary's world. It is also the Element that provides each of us with a voice; what is vision if it never finds expression? Better still, the winds behind that expression are ones that allow the Visionary to deliver his or her message wisely.

It is no coincidence that myths and legends often portray a hero trying to chase or catch the wind. What is the Visionary's quest but to catch something that before seemed impossible? The air's invisibility (but for what it affects) is like the vision or dream itself. It's often hard for anyone else to grasp but by its effects.

There are other connections between Air and the Visionary too. For example, the Bible depicts Air as fertile and filled with the power to create. A Visionary's insights can certainly be both those things. Another example comes from global cosmology, where wind gods live between heaven and Earth. Here we see how the Visionary becomes a messenger, a walker between the worlds. An interesting thing about Air is that it embodies all the other Elements in its nature, giving the Visionary ready access to the characteristics developed on the remainder of the Wheel. When the winds blow from the south, they can touch the Fires of the Warrior. When a gust comes in from the west, the Air bears the Water of the Healer. From the north, it provides the Earth of the Teacher, and from the east it bears more of the Visionary's own energies back to him or her.

Activity 7.5 - Sensing the Four Winds

This activity may take several weeks to complete, because in order to try it you will need to have an hour in which the wind is blowing from one of each of the four winds. So, if one day the wind is blowing from the south, that will be the day that you will spend an hour sensing the south wind's energy. On the day when the wind blows from the north, that will be the day you'll spend sensing the northern energies (and so forth).

When you go out into the wind, try facing it first. Extend all your senses into that onrush and ask yourself questions like:

* Is it hot, warm or cold?
* How does it taste?
* What texture does it present to your skin?
* How does it sound?
* Does it seem to have a kind of temperament (for example, angry or peaceful)?
* How does it affect the world around you? Are the trees bending? Is the grass waving?

Now, turn your back to the wind (symbolically, this means the wind is supporting you, moving you forward into energy). Ask yourself the very same questions again. Has your perception of this wind changed? Make notes of your experiences in a journal, then repeat the activity with the other three winds.

At the end of this exercise, you should feel much more intimately aware of the Air element and its characteristics. Compare those characteristics with those the Inner Visionary is trying to develop, then apply that knowledge for spell casting, ritual work, or any other mystical methods. For example, if you want to develop a strong voice, you may wish to stand in a southerly wind (the wind of power) for an hour before speaking. Or, if you want a gentle voice, turn to the Healer's wind (the west) for an hour. In this manner, the Air element and the four winds provide the Visionary with great spiritual flexibility.

Applying the Air Element

How else can each of us apply the Air element to help excite and improve our Inner Visionary? I can think of many ways including:

* Aromatherapy: Find scents that inspire you and dab them on before meditation or any spiritual undertaking.

* Breathing: There are all kinds of breathing methods that improve meditative states and help keep the Visionary centered. Explore some of them!

* Walking: The phrase "a breath of fresh air" is one worth remembering. This gives the Visionary the opportunity to breathe and think, clearing away the clutter that might impede sight.

* Wind chimes: Air has several manifestations, and one of them is to sound out the Earth's messages. Wind chimes subtly remind the Visionary of this truth.

* Wind working: Shout your needs and wishes to the winds and let that energy disperse around the world (combine those wishes with the right symbolic Element, such as Fire/south for passion).

* Stand facing a good wind and reenergize your soul, or release your burdens to the winds so that you can seek your vision without constraints.

211

* Singing: Feel the power of your words and how the Air works through you, moving out to the world. It matters little how well you sing or what you sing, just let yourself soar with sound, and words, and a tune that is your spirit.

* Honoring Air: Have a special symbolic item on your altar for the winds (maybe a winged fairy or a feather), or build a garden filled with light plants that gently sway with each wind. Honoring an Element is a great way to also get to know it more intimately.

Finally, play tag with the wind! Of all the gifts the Visionary can give himself or herself, this one may be the most necessary. A lot of the Visionary's work is serious and strenuous. Without time for play, which is also time to re-cover and rejuvenate, your inner well can easily dry up. Let the fun-loving, whimsical nature of this Element hold you and heal you until called upon by Spirit to serve yet again.

SACRED DUTY: PRAYER

"It is in vain to expect our prayers to be heard, if we do not strive as well as pray."

—Aesop

Many people have forgotten how to pray. For whatever reason, they find the whole practice uncomfortable, or feel somehow unworthy of Spirit's attention. Even the Vision-ary, who seeks to strengthen his or her connection to the Divine, often struggles with this duty.

Bringing prayer back into our daily routine is like taking a spiritual multivitamin daily: It won't do you any good if you forget! The idea here is to invite the Sacred Powers into your life 24-7, sincerely and sensibly. But for many of us, the question remains as to how to pray, or what to pray about!

Prayer has very little to do with flowery language or loudness. Instead, it's an opening of yourself and your thoughts to your image of God/dess. Such is done often with a specific theme in mind: Some prayers are requests, some are thankful, some are simply talkative, and others are worshipful. No matter the purpose, however, all prayer positively reconnects the inner Visionary and god, encouraging ongoing rapport.

Let's look at prayer multidimensionally through the archetypes. The Healer uses prayer as a way to revitalize faith and shift energy into a more positive mode in and around a person's life. The Teacher uses prayer to reconnect with and integrate important spiritual lessons. The Warrior uses prayer as a cooperative process; whatever the Warrior asks for, he or she also strives for other fronts. The Visionary rounds out this portrait by praying with an expectant, hopeful heart, one ready to receive.

Activity 7.6 - Writing a Prayer

While it might seem rather easy to write a prayer (I mean, "Dear god" qualifies), it's not quite so simple for the Inner Visionary. How does one express a desire to discover what hasn't been seen yet? How does one connect deeply when that relationship isn't presently being nourished and maintained? These are difficult questions and ones I want you to answer with total candor. Only you and Spirit are listening, so don't be shy.

As you write your Visionary's prayer, try to bring all the other archetypes into your words. Include a moment at the beginning of the prayer for the Healer's meditation to take you to the right space. Wait and use the Teacher's sense of timing to know when it is best to approach the Sacred, then use both the Teacher's and Warrior's assured voice to reveal your desire. Move out of that prayer with the Warrior's right effort, being ready to act on your request so that you remain a co-creator. And at last, use the Visionary's talent for believing in the power of our prayers and dreams to begin manifesting.

Pray for yourself; you are worthy of blessings. Pray for animals; all living things deserve to be touched by the Divine. Pray for our Earth, that she may heal. Pray for our species, that we may come to understand and honor each other's Sacred Wheel. In the words of our forbearers, "Let us pray."

Conclusion

So it is that in the still moments of the soul, talking to God/dess, the Sacred Wheel quietly turns once more, sometimes without notice. Our time of questing for a new vision passes. We found that glimmer, that piece of starlight, and not only held it in our hearts but shared it. Now it's time to take any bumps and bruises that most dreamers and thinkers inevitably endure and apply our mind toward matters of wholeness. That's right, we're back at the beginning and the end, the alpha and omega of our spiritual journey. It is time again to heal. So mote it be.

Select Bibliography

Arrien, Angeles. *The Four Fold Way*. San Francisco, CA: Harper, 1993.

Barrett, William. *Zen Budhism*. Garden City, NY: Doubleday Books, 1956.

Bruce-Mitford, Miranda. *Illustrated Book of Signs and Symbols*. DK Publishing, 1996.

Cowan, Tom. *Shamanism*. Freedom, CA: The Crossing Press, 1996.

David-Kneel, Alexandra. *Magic and Mystery in Tibet*. New York: Dover Publications, 1971.

Drury, Neevill. *The Elements of Shamanism*. Rockport, MA: Element Books, 1991.

Gordon, Stuart. *The Encyclopedia of Myths and Legends*. London: Headline,1993.

Hanh, Thich Nhat. *The Heart of the Buddha's Teaching*. New York: Broadway Books,1999.

Harner, Michael. *The Way of the Shaman*. New York: Harper Collins, 1990.

King, Serge Kahili. *Urban Shaman*. New York: Fireside Books, 1990.

Leach, Maria, ed. *Funk & Wagnall's Standard Dictionary of Folklore, Mythology, and Legend.* New York: Harper & Row, 1972.

McArthur, Margie. *The Wisdom of the Elements.* Freedom, CA: Crossing Press, 1998.

Oesterley, W.O.E. *The Sacred Dance.* Brooklyn, NY: Dance Horizons, 1923

Telesco, Patricia. *Dancing with Devas.* Lacyville, PA: Toad Hall Press, 1998.

———. *Shaman in a 9-5 World.* Freedom, CA: Crossing Press, 2000.

———. *Wicca 2000.* Secaucus, NJ: Citadel Press, 1999.

Walker, Barbara. *Woman's Dictionary of Symbols & Sacred Objects.* New York: Harper & Row, 1988.

Index

217

About the Author

Patricia Telesco is the mother of three, wife, chief human to five pets, a BBS administrator, and a full-time professional author with more than 40 metaphysical books on the market. These include, *Goddess in My Pocket*, *Kitchen Witch's Cookbook*, *Little Book of Love Magic*, *Your Book of Shadows*, *How to be a Wicked Witch*, *Charmed Life,* and other diverse titles, each of which represents a different area of spiritual interest for her and her readers. Trish considers herself a down-to-earth, militant, wooden-spoon-wielding Kitchen Witch whose love of folklore and worldwide customs flavor every spell and ritual. Although her original Wiccan education was self-trained and self-initiated, she later received initiation into the Strega tradition of Italy, which gives form and fullness to the folk magick Trish practices.

Her strongest beliefs lie in following personal vision, being tolerant of other traditions, making life an act of worship, and being creative so that magick grows with you.

Trish travels once a month to give lectures and workshops around the country. She has appeared on several television segments, including one for Sightings on mulicultural divination systems. Trish also maintains a strong presence in metaphysical journals and on the Internet through such popular sites as *www.witchvox.com* (festival focus), her home page at *www.loresinger.com*, her Yahoo! club at *www.clubs.yahoo.com/clubs/folkmagicwithtrishtelesco*, and appearances on Internet chats and bulletin boards.

Trish's hobbies include gardening, herbalism, brewing, singing, handcrafts, antique restoration, and landscaping. Her current project is helping to coordinate spiritually centered tours to Europe, and helping to support pagan land funds like that listed on *www.phoenixfestivals.com*.